gin & good guys

katrina marie

To the mamas of teens. I feel you. Also, Wee One...thank you for keeping me on track.

author's note

This book contains subjects that might be triggering. The following are included:

- Age gap relationship
- Divorce

If you want to see the content warnings of all my books, you can find it on my website.

prologue

"OW," I yell into the empty living room. Isaac's cleats are right in front of the door. I don't know how many times I've told him to put his shoes in the closet. I've tripped over them at least every other day.

"Isaac," my dad calls from the kitchen. "Get your shoes out of the middle of the floor." Huh, so he knew my son left his shoes here. He could have told him before I got home. I swear there are downsides to living with my dad. I'm just grateful he was there for me after the divorce.

He runs into the living room and scoops his cleats into his arms before dashing off to his room. "Hello, son." I don't know why I bother. It's not like he heard me. His bedroom door is closed before I'm all the way into the living room.

I set my bag on the table by the door and head toward the kitchen. "Hi, Dad."

He's cutting up cucumbers and putting them into a salad bowl filled with lettuce and other vegetables. "Hey, Bug."

"Dad, I'm grown. You don't have to call me that

anymore." Not to mention it makes no sense unless you obscure my name to be June. If they wanted to nickname me that, they shouldn't have named me Joan.

"Sorry, Bug," he glances in my direction and grins, "you'll never be too grown for me to stop with the nickname. I'm your dad, it's what we do."

"It's about as annoying as tripping over cleats when I get home." I look toward the back door. "Doesn't he have practice today?"

"Actually, it's a parent meeting. I can take him if you want me to." It's barely February. Why in the world is there already a team meeting? Plus, he has one for school sometime next month. This would be a lot easier if he'd relent and get his license. But he doesn't want to drive, despite me and his dad urging him to. Not that I could afford another car for him, or the insurance, but I'd make it work.

"No, it's fine. I'll change and get ready to go."

"You have time, Bug. Go change while I finish up dinner. We can eat before you go."

There's no use arguing with him. He doesn't like us eating a ton of fast food and prefers meals at the table. It's something we've always done no matter how late or early we'd have to eat because of school activities.

"I'll let the kids know it's almost dinner time and to get cleaned up." I take a step away from the kitchen counter. "Do both of them have practice? Or just him?"

I feel crappy for not knowing, but I'm working long hours to make sure they can do the things they love. Even if it means I can only *occasionally* catch their games.

"Just him for tonight," he continues cutting, "but tomorrow night, they both have practice. One of Abby's teammates is going to pick her up for practice and I've got Isaac."

"Thanks, Dad." I have no idea how I would handle any of this without him. After mom left, he never sought out another partner. His only focus was on raising me and making sure I got through school before releasing me into the world on my own. I don't know how I'll ever repay him...for everything.

"That's what I'm here for," he grins at me before sliding the vegetables into a bowl, "I've always got your back, Bug."

This man is ridiculous, but I wouldn't have him any other way.

* * *

There's a meeting every season, but this is the first time I've been able to make it. My dad usually brings him, or his dad does. Almost every single kid has both parents in attendance. A small part of me wishes Keith was here so I wouldn't feel out of my element, but he had a dinner meeting. Though, having him here would defeat the purpose of proving to myself I can do these things on my own.

When we were together, he handled most of the sports things. I kept up with the calendar and made sure we were there for practices and game days. Back then I was able to do that because I wasn't working insane hours just to provide for them. I'm sure Keith would give more in child support, but I can't ask that of him. He already goes above and beyond. My friends said we'd never be able to co-parent in a healthy way, but we can. And we are. It took both of us too many years to realize we had become roommates instead of a couple.

"Thanks for coming tonight," the coach breaks into my thoughts, "we won't be here long. I just want to go over the upcoming schedule and fees for the summer."

His wife hands out stapled packets. Isaac is looking over my shoulder to read. Everything is pretty standard with previous years, except when I get to the amount. It's a good thing Isaac can't see my expression. One look and he'd want to quit to keep me from stressing out.

I glance around the room, and I'm happy to see I'm not the only one with sticker shock. A couple of other parents are flipping to the other pages to see why the amount is so much.

The coach must have sensed what the room is feeling because he speaks again, "I know it's more than last year, but the prices of everything are going up. The uniforms went up the most, and we have a few tournaments we'll be traveling a few hours away to attend."

One brave parent raises his hand. "Do we need the full amount up front?"

"The only thing we need up front is the uniforms," Coach glances down at the paper. "I have the cost of every-thing broken down if you flip to the next page," he takes a deep breath, "ideally, we'd like as many to pay the full amount as possible, but we know not everyone can do that. If you need to make a payment plan, you can see me, or my wife, after the meeting."

The parent who asked nods. But I don't miss his gulp, as he takes in the information.

I turn the page and study the breakdown. It's nice to see where exactly the money is going. It doesn't cure the small panic attack I'm having, though. I don't know how I'm going to pay for this. I can't ask his dad. He's already agreed to pay for school uniforms next school year.

Asking my dad is completely out of the question. He already does so much for us, and charges peanuts in rent just so I can do fun things with the kids when I'm off work.

The coach goes over more information, but I'm barely paying attention. The options I have are very few. I'll have to get a second job, which means even less time with the kids. Being a single mom feels like an impossible task, and I'm beginning to wonder if I'm cut out for it.

"Again, thank y'all for coming. We're going to have a great baseball season against some pretty tough teams. I know these boys can do it, though." He pauses for a second, "guys, y'all can grab some snacks my wife made, and start thinking about some fundraising you want to do."

Well, that part completely flew over my head. At least, we'll have that to fall back on. But I'm not sure how much they'll actually raise. Times are hard for everyone.

Standing I make my way to the tables Coach and his wife are sitting at. There's a signup sheet for snacks after games. I silently groan because that is more money. Not that the boys don't deserve it, but this is...a lot.

I pull a check out of my wallet so I'm prepared when it's my turn. Now I just have to figure out how I'll come up with the rest of the money.

* * *

"Dad," I call out after the kids have gone to bed. He doesn't answer, and I'm beginning to wonder if he called it a night as well. He's the resident night owl, so it would be weird.

"Yeah, Bug?" He comes into the living room from the attached garage.

"Can you watch the kids later than usual the next couple of weeks?" I have my laptop resting on my knees, staring at the site in front of me.

"Sure," he shrugs and takes a seat on the sofa beside me, "what's up?"

"I'm going to bartender school." It's the quickest way I know to make fast cash. If I can find a job at a busy bar, I'll be able to pay for Isaac's baseball, and Abby's summer volleyball, in no time.

"Why?" I can hear the disapproval in his voice. But it's not going to deter me. "If you need money, I can give it to you."

"I know," I lean my head against his shoulder, "this is something I need to do on my own."

He doesn't say anything for a few moments, and I worry I've upset him more than I realize. Finally, he sighs. "If that's what you feel you need to do, I'll support you."

"Thanks, Dad." The class isn't too expensive. I only hope I can find a job quickly after I'm certified.

1

eric

LISA AND DELILAH are motioning me to come inside the bar. My break is over, and they need help. If only I could get my mom off the phone.

"Are you listening to me?" Mom's voice is loud in the mostly quiet parking lot.

"Yes, Mom," I shake my head and hold up my hand, hoping they understand I need a few more minutes, "I'm listening."

"I should have his schedule by the end of next week."

Wait. What? Maybe I wasn't listening as closely as I should have been. "What schedule?"

"I knew it," she huffs. Great, now I've pissed her off. She won't be mad long, but she will make comments about it for the next few days. "Your brother has summer practices. I know it's early, but I'll need your help getting him there and back. Can you do that for me?"

Wow. Talk about getting started early. There's still a

month and a half of school left. "Yeah, it shouldn't be a problem."

"It's all during the day, and I know you work mostly nights," she pauses for a second. "If you can't just let me know, and I'll figure something out."

"You don't have to do that, Mom." I lean against the brick wall. The air is thick and I have a feeling it's going to rain soon. It's probably why the bar is packed tonight, even though it's during the week. "I can get him there."

"Thank you," she breathes a sigh of relief. "If he keeps joining activities, I'll have to get a second job to support them."

"Don't worry about that." If she needs anything, I've got it. I know she doesn't like it, but this is one of those times she needs to push aside her pride. Maybe I should text Cameron and ask him if she's already paid for this summer conditioning thing. "I'll handle whatever comes up."

"Who's the parent here? I'm supposed to take care of the two of you, not the other way around."

"You already took care of me, Mom. Let me repay the favor." It's a battle she won't let go, but she doesn't turn down the money I shift to her account every month. "My break is over. I need to get back to work."

"Okay. Call me tomorrow?"

"I will as soon as I wake up." As if I don't talk to her almost daily.

"Love you. Be careful on your way home."

"Love you, too, Mom." Before she has a chance to say anything else, I press the end button.

She'll keep me on the phone for hours without saying anything of importance. I get it. It wasn't that long ago that I moved out of her house. She's used to having me around, and this is her way of doing that.

Shoving the phone in my pocket, I head toward the door. There's a group of people blocking it, and I have to maneuver my way through them to open it.

Delilah nods at me as I walk in. "Better hurry before Lisa loses it."

"On it." Lisa is still pretty new to bartending and large crowds overwhelm her. She's so focused on getting the drinks right, that she can't pay attention to all the customers hollering their orders over the music.

"Finally," she throws her hands in the air, "you can't leave me like that back here. I know what I'm doing, but not at the pace you usually serve."

"You're doing great, Lisa," I motion toward the people crowded around the bar, "do you see anyone complaining?"

She shakes her head and continues pouring a beer. "But—"

"But nothing," I start on the customer closest to me, "most of the folks here are regulars, and they know you're still getting the hang of things."

"I guess." She slides the drink across the bar and asks the next customer what they'll have.

We work as fast as we can to get the customer's drinks. It takes about fifteen minutes, but it's fine because it keeps me busy and less focused on my mom's financial problems. I can't imagine the stress she's feeling, though I was hoping a lot of it would go away when I moved out. One less mouth to feed and all that.

Most would argue it's not my job to help, but I can't do that to her. She's, my mom. Aside from my friends, her and my brother are all I have. Our dad isn't winning any parent of the year awards, and I'll do everything in my power to make sure they are living as comfortably as possible. And for Cameron to do all the things he wants without worrying about how mom is going to pay for it.

* * *

The bar is officially closed. One of the perks of working during the week. We close early. Inventory needs to be done before I can leave for the night, though.

Most of the staff is gone. Delilah and Lisa are the only people left. The two of them always go above and beyond to help when they are on a shift with me.

Delilah is walking around the bar doing a last-minute check. It makes opening a lot easier, but I hardly work those shifts anymore. Carlos and Angie usually cover those since they both have partners and families.

She makes her way to the bar counter and leans against it. "If that's everything, I think I'm going to head out."

"You're good," I nod toward the door, "go home and get some rest. Be careful, it felt like it was going to storm when I was outside earlier."

"Pfft. I'm always careful." She waves and heads toward the front door. Lisa follows behind her to lock it up.

I scan the shelves to see what we need to restock. The whiskey was flowing tonight and I'll have to check the back room to make sure we have plenty for the upcoming weekend. The live music means we go through more alcohol than we used to.

Grabbing a pen and notepad off the countertop, I make a note of the liquor we'll need to restock. It probably wouldn't hurt to order more syrups as well. But I'd rather do this than dwell on the thought of my mom getting another job to support my brother.

"Is everything okay?" Lisa rounds the bar before checking the coolers. "You look like you're deep in thought."

"I'm good. Just making lists."

"Nice try, buddy. Can't bullshit a bullshitter." She closes the cooler and leans against it, waiting for me to say something.

She's not wrong. She's also probably the only person I'd consider talking to about everything going on. When we were roommates, we quickly became best friends. It's not her problem, though.

"Just some stuff with my mom."

"Want to talk about it?" She moves and looks through the stock on her side of the bar. Being still is not something she does often.

Shaking my head, even though she can't see me, I mumble, "not really."

"I'm here if you need anything." She will be, too.

I need to lighten the mood, though. I don't want her worrying about what's going on with me. "Anything?"

She stops what she's doing and side-eyes me. "That depends," she studies me for a few seconds, "why do I have a feeling I'm not going to like whatever you're about to ask me?"

She probably won't be happy, but I'm going to shoot my shot, anyway. "When are you going to bring your bartender friend around?"

"Seriously? We're doing that again?" She rolls her eyes and continues going through the stock.

"What's so wrong with me asking?" The paper thuds and the pen clatters as I toss them on the counter. "She's single, I'm single. Maybe we can be single together."

"Dude," Lisa sighs, "she's way older than you and has two kids."

"I like kids." It's a little weird she's using that as an excuse. "I throw the ball around with David all the time. He's like my little best friend. Aside from you, of course."

"They are *teens*, Eric." She says it as if that says everything I need to know.

"So is my brother," I wave my hand in the air. "I fail to see the problem here." She's making this a much bigger deal than it needs to be.

"Look," she stops going through the shelves and turns toward me, "I love you. You know that, right?"

"Yes," I draw out.

"I just don't want either of you getting hurt." She picks up a towel and absent-mindedly wipes down the countertop, "she hasn't been out of her marriage long, and she's going to apply to work here. The last thing I need is for y'all to hit it off for a few nights and then make things awkward here when we're working."

Talk about a punch to the gut. Without saying the actual words, I see how she feels about me. "Geez, don't hold back."

"That's not what I mean, Eric." She moves toward me, leaving the towel behind, "I know more than anyone you're a massive flirt. How many people have you taken home in the past month? She has kids to worry about."

"First of all, I've only taken like two women home." I hold up one finger to make my point. Then another one. "Secondly, she's an adult. I'm an adult. How about we let her make her own decisions?"

"You know what? You're right." She holds her hands in the air, "the both of you can decide what to do if she comes around again." She grabs the notepad I set on the counter and heads toward the hallway that leads to the office. "Just don't put me in the middle."

Other areas of my life may be falling apart, but all I heard is there's a shot. That tiny bit of hope is all I need.

2

joan

"MOM!"

I swear this is the tenth time my name has been yelled from across the house since I've been home. I don't bother yelling back. It drives me up the wall when the kids do it, and maybe if I show them the proper way to converse with me, they'll mimic. I feel like it's a lost cause at this point, though.

At least I'm not tripping over equipment as I make my way down the hall to my son's room. "Yes, Isaac, what is it you need?"

He jumps, and I stifle a laugh. "I didn't realize you were right freaking there."

"I wasn't. I walked in here to talk to you like a normal person." Leaning against the door frame, I take in his room. It needs to be cleaned, but it's not as bad as it usually is. "What do you need?"

"Have you seen my cleats?" The plus side is I know they aren't in the middle of the floor because I didn't trip over them. The downside...I haven't seen them. "My teammate will be here any minute and I need them for practice."

"Did you look in your closet? Or, even the hall closet?"

He shakes his head vehemently. I bet he didn't even look. "They aren't in there. It's the first place I checked."

"Did you ask Grandpa? He may have moved them somewhere."

"That's a good idea." He rushes past me in search of my dad. I seriously doubt my dad had anything to do with his cleats going missing, but it's worth a shot.

I take a few steps into his room and glance around the floor. Then check his closet. He may have looked, but probably not thoroughly. He's right, though. They aren't in his closet. There's only one more place they can be.

I get on my knees and bend over until I'm eye level with the space under his bed. Lifting the bed skirt, I prepare myself for the mess I'll find under here. There isn't anything shoved into the small space. Well, except for two things. I grab his shoes and pull them out from under his bed before standing up.

"He said he doesn't know where they are." Before he has a chance to freak out more than he already is, I dangle his cleats in front of me. "Thanks, Mom. You saved me from having to run laps around the field."

"You're welcome." I open my arms up for a hug, and he awkwardly wraps one arm around me for a few seconds before pulling away. I miss the days when he would hug me for no reason other than being his mom. I guess he's *too old* for that now. "Do I need to pick you up from practice?"

"Nope. I have a ride." He takes his cleats and rushes toward the door, grabbing his bat bag on the way. "I'll see you when I get home."

"Be careful, and have fun." I call after him. He didn't

hear me, though. The front door slammed shut before I even got the sentence out. That kid is quick.

I pick up the dirty laundry scattered in front of his bed and put it in the laundry basket. He can tackle that when he gets home. He's lucky it was only his school clothes on the floor because I'm not a fan of picking up his clothes after practice. It's gross.

Leaving his room, I close the door behind me and head to the kitchen. His baseball schedule will most likely eat up our weekends, and I need to let Carlos know when I'll be able to work.

"Mom," here we go again, "can you help me with my homework?"

"That depends," I set the schedule on the bar and turn toward Abby, "what subject?"

"Algebra," she sets her laptop, and some paper, on the table. "I don't understand it. And the teacher sucks at explaining it."

"Did you ask them for help?"

"No," she grunts, "it wouldn't matter. If I don't under-stand how she explains it to the class, what difference would it make if I ask her on my own?"

"That's a pretty flimsy excuse. I'm sure she would have tried to help you in a way it makes sense for you." I pull out the chair next to where she set her stuff down. "But I'll give it my best shot."

Twenty minutes. That's how long we spend on her homework before I throw my hands in the air. "I don't understand the way they have y'all doing math. No wonder you don't get it."

"No offense, Mom, but the way you do it is so much harder than the way we do."

"If you say so," I mutter under my breath, "want to help me get dinner ready?"

"Actually, I'm going to call Chloe and see if she can help me with the homework." She gathers her things and heads toward the living room.

"Make sure it's actually help, and not just giving you the answers."

"I know." She leaves the kitchen with her phone already in her hand. Fingers moving rapidly over the screen.

Leaning back, I grab Isaac's schedule off the bar. His school games are already in my calendar. I just need to add these.

After this weekend, I'll be able to pay the balance for his select team. I still have a couple more weeks, but I want to get it taken care of sooner than later. Thank God for the tips I get as a bartender. Now I can start saving up for a car for him.

"What are you doing, Bug?" My dad pulls out a chair and sits.

"Syncing up my calendar with the newest schedule." I sigh as I see the days filling up. Most of the games are in the morning and afternoon. Which is good because it means I'll still be able to work nights at the bar.

"That sounds like fun," he leans back, "are you adding them to the calendar all of us share?"

"Yep." With each event I add, I know it's making the kids' phones blow up. Isaac won't be annoyed by it until he's done with practice, but Abby...I know she's probably silently cursing me.

"Don't forget about the game this week. If you want to meet us there, I can take him. It's one less stop you have to make."

I hate relying on my dad so much. I'm grown, I should have my shit figured out. "That sounds good."

"Good," he stands and goes to the fridge, "I'll get dinner started."

"I can do that, Dad." I scoot the chair back, prepared to stop him, "I was about to until I got distracted by the schedule."

"No, you sit," he motions for me to stay where I am. "You worked today. All I did was play a round of golf while the kids were in school."

"Retirement looks good on you, old man."

He flexes his muscle as he sets the eggs on the bar. Looks like it's breakfast for dinner, my favorite. "Who are you calling old?"

I laugh and turn back toward the table. There are times I wonder what went through my mom's head when she left us. Dad is funny, sweet, and most things women want in a man. I stop my thoughts in their tracks. Going down the road of *what ifs* won't do me any good.

I set the schedule down and open up one of the word games on my phone. This is how I'll spend the time until dinner is ready. Hopefully Isaac will be home by then, and we won't have to reheat anything. Right now, though...I'll take the blissful quiet.

* * *

"You look exhausted. Why don't you take a break, and I'll cover your area of the bar for a bit."

Carlos is well-intentioned, but damn. He didn't have to call me out like that. He's not wrong. Multiple games during the week are taking its toll on me.

"I'm good." A customer approaches the bar asking for a

beer on tap, and I rush to get his drink for him. "Do you want to start a tab?"

"Sure," he smiles up at me and slides his card across the counter, "I'll be back."

"You got it." I head to the computer and put in his information.

"Watch out for that guy." I know who it is before I turn around.

"Who?"

"The order you just took." Eric points to the man carrying his beer around the corner where a local band is setting up to play, "he's hit on all the bartenders."

"Including you?" I smirk, knowing it will get a rise out of him.

"No," he scoffs, "but now I'm offended he hasn't." He puts a hand over his chest as if he's heartbroken by the thought.

"Maybe you aren't his type."

He shrugs, "maybe. I'm just looking out for you."

"Jealousy doesn't look good on you," I sing song as I walk away. I may be exhausted, but I know what he's trying to do. He's made no secret of trying to get a date with him. He's even gone as far as to get Lisa to vouch for him.

"I'm not jealous." He clears his throat and walks off to another area of the bar.

As if I can't see through his words. I'm pretty sure I'm over a decade older than him, and I've seen this before when I was his age. Not with me personally, but with other people.

"Joan, your phone is vibrating all over the shelf in the office," Lisa says as she rounds the back of the bar. "You may want to see what it's about."

She's right. Even though my dad is watching the kids,

something could have happened and I'm almost an hour away from them. "Can you cover my area?"

"I got you," she grins and heads to a space between both our areas. She's already taking an order before I've made it to the hallway.

There's a line forming in the hall for the restrooms, and I maneuver between people to get to the office door. I knock before trying the handle. I heard Eric walked in on Lisa making out with her boyfriend one time and I don't want to be that person.

"Come in." The door and loud music muffle Carlos's voice.

I turn the knob and ease my way into the spacious room. "Sorry. Lisa said my phone is ringing nonstop."

"No worries," he points to the phone which is ringing...again. "Looks like you're taking that break anyway," he laughs and stands up from behind the desk, "I'll give you some privacy."

"Thanks." I wave at him as he vacates the room.

My phone has stopped ringing and I check the call log. Ten missed calls from Abby. Whatever it is, it can't be good if she's blowing up my phone like this.

I press her number and wait for it to ring. She answers after the first one. "Finally. I've been trying to call you."

"I'm at work. I don't keep my phone on me." I don't feel the need to have it on me twenty-four seven like these kids today. Maybe it's from growing up without one, I don't know. But I don't typically carry it in my pocket. "Is every-thing okay?"

"Maybe you should." She pauses for a second before speaking again, "Isaac won't stop coming into my room and bugging me and Chloe."

Seriously? This is what she calls me for. I thought something may have happened with the way she was calling me. Take a breath. Nothing good will come out of losing my shit on her. "Can you please put your brother on the phone?"

She yells his name and I hold the phone away from my ear. Less than a minute later, he says "Hello?"

"Please leave the girls alone."

"She really called to snitch on me?" I can hear his sigh over the phone and I know he is going to retaliate at some point. I'm not going to worry about that now.

"It doesn't matter." A headache is forming and it's not from the music, or lack of sleep. Parenting two kids is hard as hell. Doing it while single and working insane hours adds to the stress. "Just leave them alone. Go hang out with Grandpa or something."

"No teenager wants to hang out with their grandpa on a Friday night." My dad says something in the background, but I can't hear him. "I'll leave them alone."

"Thank you." When I'm sure he's not going to say anything else, I ask him to put his sister back on the phone. "Abby, I love you and if there's an actual emergency I'll be on my way. But please figure out how to settle these issues, or take it to Grandpa. He's the one at home."

"But—"

"No buts," I sigh, "just steer clear of your brother and listen to Grandpa. I'll see you in the morning."

"Okay. Love you and be careful coming home."

"Love you, too." I hang up before she adds some other grievance against her brother.

There's a knock on the door before Carlos pokes his head inside. "Sorry to ask you to cut your break short, but the crowd is picking up out there. We need all hands on-deck."

"No worries, I'm done." I set my phone back on the shelf and make my way toward the door.

"Is everything okay?"

"Teenagers." That's all I can think to say. I know he doesn't have kids, and his girlfriend's son is still pretty young, but he's in for a rude awakening.

3

eric

THE CROWD TONIGHT IS WILD. There's a new band playing on the regular since Lisa's boyfriend is off touring with Crooked Halo. This new band plays a slightly harder and brings in folks that can be a little rambunctious.

My eyes track Joan as she exits the hall and takes her place behind the bar. A small part of me is still annoyed because she thinks I'm jealous.

Okay, I may be a tiny bit jealous. I'll never admit it, though. She needed to be warned, though. That guy started coming in here a few weeks ago, and has made it a point to hit on all the women on my team.

He's polite, but it's the way he talks to them and how he leans over the bar to get as close as he can that creeps me out.

I may be persistent in my date requests of Joan, but I don't think I make her feel uncomfortable. At least, I hope I don't. And if I do, I want her to tell me. Because that shit is not cool. I never want to make anyone feel that way.

That guy in particular is definitely bad news, though. Lisa goes out of her way to keep from serving him, and she gets along with everyone. This is the first time he's come on a weekend, and I don't want him taking advantage of Joan's kindness. Not if I can help it.

More and more people filter through the door, and I know it's going to be a long night.

A lady slides her way between two people and leans over the bar. She seems to be around the same age as Joan, but I suck at being able to tell anyone's age. Her lowcut shirt exposes the tops of her breasts, and I do my best to keep my focus on her eyes. "Hey handsome, can I get a vodka tonic?"

Before Joan caught my interest, I totally would have flirted right back. But I don't want her to think I'm a fuck boy. At least, not anymore. "Sure thing. I'll have it right up."

The vodka is on the other side of the bar and I have to walk past Joan to get to it. Maybe she didn't see the interaction between me and the customer. Not that I did anything wrong, but still.

My steps are quick as I make my way behind her to grab the bottle of vodka. I'm not even past her before she catches my eye and smirks. "You should probably watch out for that one. I know the look of a cougar going in for the kill."

"It's not like that." And how would she know? I wasn't under the impression she was dating. If she is, why won't she give me the time of day. I do my best to ignore the dig, and grab the bottle a couple of feet from where she's standing.

"If you say so," she sing-songs as I make my way back to my area. I should be thrilled she actually talked to me. Not that she doesn't normally, but I'm the one who has to start the conversation and she's pretty quick to end it. You'd think I'd get the hint and leave it be. My mom always says I'm stubborn, and this is proof.

I make quick work of the vodka tonic and slide it over the bar with a napkin. "Here you go. Is there anything else I can get you?"

She hands me her card and grins. "Why don't you start a tab for me? I'll be back to see you." She winks before turning to disappear into the crowd. I don't miss her glance back, or the way she shifts her dress an inch or two higher.

Please do not let her come back to my side of the bar. Joan may be right. I mean, there's nothing wrong with this woman. She's gorgeous, but I don't necessarily want to go home with her.

There's only one person I want anything to do with, and she's shooting daggers at me. Great. Now what did I do?

I make my way toward her, but Lisa intercepts me. "That's probably not a good idea."

"Why? I didn't do anything wrong, and it's not like we're dating or anything."

Lisa only shakes her head in response. "Not everything is about you, Eric. Sometimes family shit comes up and messes with a person's mood."

She's preaching to the choir. My brother's camp fees are due next week, and I'll be sending any tips I make to my mom to cover it.

"Just give her some space," she pours a drink, "nobody likes to be pressured into a date."

"Hmph, tell that to basically all of our friends who have gotten into relationships lately." I don't bother telling her she's included in that. Besides, I don't like to think of it as pressuring. I'm taking my shot. It's just taking more shots than I anticipated.

She doesn't argue with me because she knows it's true. Every single person who is in a relationship met, or got together, because of this place. Why is it so bad, for me to do the same?

"I'm not saying back off completely on your quest," she places her hands on my shoulders, "I'm only saying that you should dampen your excitement. It's kind of a lot."

The grin that spreads across my face likely looks maniacal, I'm sure. If she meant that as a slam, she failed. My mom always said I'm extra when it comes to challenges.

"I just added gasoline to the fire, didn't I?" She crosses her arms and sizes me up.

"That is something you'll have to wait and see." I wave at her and go down to the far end of the bar. She can manage the middle while I figure out my next move.

* * *

The last patrons are walking out the door, and we can *finally* start our clean up routine. It's been a long night. Not only did that woman keep coming to me for drinks, she slipped her phone number at the bottom of the receipt. Nice try, lady, but my eyes are set on another.

I wipe down the counter in my section and can't help but replay all the times that troublemaker came to the bar to hit on Joan. Is it fair to call him that? Maybe not, but I've seen him do the same thing all week to every one of our bartenders. With any luck, one of them will mention it to her, so it doesn't seem like I'm jealous.

Which I'm totally not. Well, not completely. I watch Lisa talk to her as I continue cleaning the counter, and I wish I could hear what they are talking about. Lisa has definitely perfected the art of talking quietly. Something I've never been able to do. Being subtle isn't one of my strengths.

My coworkers are trying to get the tables and floor clean in the main areas, and I need to help them. That would require me to pass by Lisa and Joan. Now's my chance to hear what they're saying. I toss the rag in the bucket to be washed and take slow, steady steps toward them. Joan's eyes meet mine, and she immediately stops talking until I'm on the other side of the bar and heading toward the tables.

All that tells me is they were talking about me. Or, at least, something that pertains to me. Hopefully Lisa wasn't warning her away. Especially after I had her vouch for me when Joan first started working here.

"You get that side and I get this one?" Delilah nods toward the other side of the room. "I'm ready to get out of here and head home."

"Oh yeah? I'm guessing Bryce is waiting for you?" I'm glad they have each other. I don't think she would have given him the time of day if I hadn't nudged them together any chance I could.

"If he knows what's best for him, he'll be asleep and I can crash as soon as I get home."

"My fingers are crossed for you." I laugh as I grab one of the rags she has next to her, "or else you'll be up for whatever movie marathon he has planned for you."

"Don't even speak that into existence."

I hold my hands up in surrender as I back away. "I take it all back. He'll be asleep and you can go to bed."

"That's better." She grins and wipes down the table in front of her. I watch how she does the cleanup for a second. She doesn't put the chairs up immediately after she wipes the table. Instead, she wipes down several tables and then goes back to do the chairs. Not the way I would do it, but to each their own.

The sooner we get this done the sooner we can get out of here. I have to be at my mom's early in the morning, and I'd like to get as much sleep as I possibly can. Helping her get my brother back and forth to things is exhausting, but at least it's benefiting her. She doesn't have to take time off work, or worry about getting an additional job as long as I'm around.

"Hey," Joan's voice jolts me out of my thoughts and I jump up from wiping the table, inches from our heads colliding, "didn't mean to scare you."

"Sorry, did you need something?" This is the first time she's approached me and I hope like hell it's personal. Even if I'm almost certain it's not.

"I was just seeing if it's okay for me to head out. Everything is cleared up and put away." Her phone is in her hand and she looks nervous to be asking.

"Sure, is everything okay?" Surely, she would have asked earlier if it was an emergency.

She lifts her head up, staring at the ceiling and sighs. "Yeah, for the most part. But these kids are pushing all of my buttons today." She finally brings her attention back to me, "sorry, that was totally unprofessional."

"It's okay." I hold up my hands, "I may not have kids, but I know how hard it can be with teens."

Her head tilts to the side. "How?"

"I have a little brother. He's in high school, and as much as I'd like to say I'm the cool older brother, I don't understand what he's talking about half the time."

"Ah, so we're in the same boat."

I shrug, "pretty much. But if you need to go, that's

completely okay." I watch her type out something on her phone. "You have the shift for tomorrow night, right?"

"Uh huh." She's not paying much attention as she heads toward the door, but she stops as if someone just hit the brakes. "Actually, I may be a tad bit late. My son has games tomorrow, and they should be done before I have to come in. But, you know, just in case I'm not here early, you know what's going on."

"No problem," I wave her toward the door. This is my shot to ask her to dinner. But she's out the door before I can say another word. "Damn it."

Lisa comes up behind me and pats me on the shoulder. "Smooth."

"Shut up," I push her hand away, "what was I supposed to do? If I would have asked her on a date when she clearly had her hands full with her kids, I would have looked like an asshole."

"You're not wrong there." She grabs my arm and pulls me toward the bar, "for someone who is a notorious flirt, you aren't so great at it when it comes to Joan."

"Whatever." Our coworkers are filing out the front door, and I pull out a barstool, taking a seat. "What would you have done?"

"I literally warned you away from asking her out a few hours ago, and now you're asking for my advice?"

"I'm a glutton for punishment."

"Maybe don't try to relate to her so hard. I know you think you're on the same footing because you help your mom with your brother, but you're not. You get to go home at the end of the day. She doesn't."

"So, I'm supposed to just be myself?" Sighing, I run a hand through my hair, "that hasn't worked so far. I figured I would switch it up."

"Yeah, don't do that. She'll either come around, or she won't." She pats my shoulder and heads toward the door. "I think you may have finally found someone resistant to your charm." And with that my best friend walks out the door. She definitely knows how to make an exit.

Hmph. It will be a cold day in hell before I ever admit I've met my match.

4

joan

TEN MINUTES until I have to clock in, and I'm five minutes away. My fingers tap, tap, tap against the steering wheel while I wait for this stupid light to turn green. There isn't even anyone at the other lights. While I enjoy the smalltown vibe, I don't love the traffic situation. It's worse than the city in some ways.

Finally, the light I've been stuck at for what seems like ages is green. As much as I want to haul ass through this light and town to get to work, I don't need a speeding ticket on my record. Not when I'm about to begin driving lessons with Isaac.

Everyone in town must be at the bar and their own sporting events because the traffic is light as I make my way to Out of the Ashes. Could I have gotten a job closer to home? Probably. But I don't think the work environment would have been quite as laid back as it is here.

Pulling into the parking lot, I glance at the time. Two

minutes. I'm cutting it close. Being to work a minimum of fifteen minutes early is something I always strive for, but I couldn't make that happen today. Isaac's game was delayed because the one prior to it went into overtime. Being a sports mom isn't for the faint of heart.

I throw the car in park before turning it off and grabbing my phone and wallet. The wind catches the door as I swing it open and I have to hurl myself at it to keep it from hitting the car next to me. Another expense I definitely do not need.

My phone is vibrating in my hand as I press the button to lock the car. I swear if it's one of the kids, I might scream. The phone stops vibrating for two seconds and starts again. A quick glance at the phone, and I sigh as I swipe across the screen. "Please tell me you aren't already fighting."

"Abby won't give me the charger and my phone is about to die." They act like it's the end of the world if their phone dies. I remember a time when we didn't have phones glued to our hands. But, alas, the advancement of technology has hit us full force.

"Aren't you at your dad's?"

"Yes," the word is drawn out through the speaker, as if it just dawned on him, "I should probably go to him, huh?"

"Yes, you should." I stop at the front door to finish the conversation. "You're over there until Monday evening after practice. Unless it's an emergency, go to your dad. Well, if it's an emergency, too, but not for stuff like this. I'm late for work."

"Sorry, Mom," he pauses for a second, "I'll talk to Dad. Have a good night at work, and be careful on your way home."

"I will." A small smile creeps across my face. They may

annoy the crap out of me sometimes, but I always miss them when they are gone. "Have fun at your dad's, love you."

"Love you, too." He doesn't say bye before hanging up the phone. It's one of my pet peeves, and something I hope he'll grow out of.

Before tucking my phone away in my back pocket, I shoot off a text to Abby.

Mom: Have fun this weekend. And please don't fight with your brother.

I don't wait for a response. If I know my daughter, she's rolling her eyes and making faces at Isaac for calling me. There will probably be a smartass text waiting on me when I go on break.

Opening the door, I slide past the people waiting on a table. I don't know why they bother. There's plenty of standing room around the dance floor. But I guess Patrick is still technically cooking dinner items instead of bar snacks.

Waving at Carlos and Eric, I holler, "I'm putting my stuff away and I'll be right out."

"Take your time," Eric answers, "you have time."

Slowing, I take in the spaces open at the bar. He's right. Good. I'll have time to do something with my hair before I come out.

I open the office door and close it behind me. I set my stuff on one of the shelves and glance in the mirror hanging on the wall. Good God. No wonder Eric said I have time. The pieces of hair that fell out of my ponytail are sticking in every direction. My cheeks are tinged pink from the sun. Hopefully that's as bright as it gets and I didn't get an actual sunburn.

Another trip to the car is in order. I keep an emergency

brush in the console. I can't do much about my makeup, but I can at least make sure my hair is presentable. Moving toward the door, I step back when it swings open.

"Wh-what are you doing back here?" Eric is staring at me. Is it good, or bad? I can't tell.

He shakes himself out of whatever trance he was in and opens the door farther. I have no clue why, but I'm not questioning it. "I was coming to see if you needed anything."

Leaning back, I take another quick glance in the mirror. I really don't want to go back out there looking like a mess. "Actually, wanna do me a favor?"

"Sure." He shrugs. His almost black hair falling into his face. "What do ya need?"

"There's a brush in the console of my car." I hold my keys out, "any chance you can grab it for me? I don't want to scare off potential customers."

"I doubt you'd scare them off," he smirks and reaches for the keys. "I'll be right back."

"Thanks," I call out, but the door is already closing behind him. Lisa was right about one thing: he goes out of his way to help people. I can't help but wonder if his motivation is purely out of kindness, or a way to keep showing his interest in me. Probably best not to question it. He's keeping me from having to go into the bar area looking like I got attacked by Mother Nature, even if that's exactly what happened at the game.

I move back to the mirror and pull the scrunchie out my hair when the door opens again. "Here you go." He stops behind me and holds the brush over my shoulder.

"Thank you." I wait for him to go back to the bar, but he doesn't move. "Is there anything else?"

"You should wear your hair down more often." He reaches toward a frizzy strand but pulls away at the last second. "It looks good."

That's not exactly what I'd call it, but okay. "I feel like it gets in the way when I'm making drinks."

"I can understand that." His hair isn't long. It reminds me of those emo pop bands from when I was in my late teens.

"Can you, though?" I smile and point to his hair then mine. "Mine is a lot longer than what you have."

"You have a point." He takes a step back noticing the closeness between us. A teeny tiny part of me wishes he would have moved in the opposite direction. "I should probably get back out there before Carlos thinks we're doing something we shouldn't be in here."

"What do you mean?"

"If you only knew how many of our fellow coworkers have been caught making out in here at various times." The way he's looking at me makes me think he wouldn't be opposed to being another one of those employees.

I'll take that decision out of his hands. "I'll, uh, see you out there in a bit. I'm just gonna—" I point toward my hair.

"Yeah, sure. See you." He turns and walks out the door, closing it behind him.

Deep breath in and out. I wasn't lying when I told Lisa I think he's attractive. In any other universe I'd take a chance with him. But right now...it's just not in the cards. There's already too much on my plate and adding a guy to the mix isn't something I should even be considering.

* * *

"Hey, Eric," I call across the bar, "can you hand me the tequila?" We're almost out on this side of the bar, and I need to make this margarita.

He grabs the bottle from the shelf, and I think he's going to walk it over. Instead, he slides it across the counter to me, earning cheers from the customers. He's such a show off. The customers love him, though.

"Need anything else?" He waggles his eyebrows up and down. I know it's supposed to be seductive, but it's adorable.

Shit. No. Not adorable. I shouldn't be feeling any kind of way about him. "I'm good, thanks."

There. That should diminish how much he's flirting with me. His answering smirk tells me otherwise. I've never met anyone quite like him. He has these moments where he's sweet and caring, like he was when I was freshening up after the game. Then there's the cocky version everyone gets when he's behind this counter. Which act is real? This is why I don't know if I could ever take him seriously.

The music is blaring and I can see people dancing to the band. There's only about thirty minutes left of serving alcohol. I slide the margarita to the woman in front of me and she asks me to close out her tab. The time to wind down has begun.

After she's done paying, I take advantage of the lull in customers on my side of the bar and wipe down the counters. Anything to make the cleanup go faster once we close. My body is exhausted after spending all day in the sun only to come to work for hours on my feet.

It's worth it, though. Seeing my kids enjoy the things they love, and being able to pay for it without help from Keith or my dad is the cherry on the sundae.

My break is short-lived as people come up to the bar to

pay their bills before heading home for the night. One after the other takes care of their tab. Eric is using the computer on his side to cash people out, but he's faster. I'll get the hang of everything…eventually.

The last of the customers are walking out the door, and the band is clearing off the stage. I start the bar breakdown process I learned in class. I also make a note to restock the tequila tomorrow since I don't work on Sunday. It's my one day off, and my bed is calling my name. Nothing will pull me away from it except maybe food.

I'm almost done cleaning my area when I feel Eric standing behind me. Should I know what his presence feels like? Probably not, but after the moment we shared in the office, it's there just the same.

"So, uh, what are you doing after you leave here?" As cocky as he usually sounds, when I turn around, he seems nervous. His hands are shoved in his back pockets, and his eyes are directed just over my head.

I set down the rag and lean against the counter. "Going home. It's been a long day."

"Oh." His shoulders sag and he turns toward the other end of the bar.

A small part of me wants to know what he wants. "Why? What's up?" Maybe he needs help with something here at the bar and he was wondering if I could stay late. That's the only thing I can think of even though I know he likes me. There's no way he actually might want to ask me on a date.

"There's a small get together at Lisa's house, and I was wondering if you're going. She said she was going to text you, but she probably forgot. She's not married to her phone like most of us."

He's not wrong there. She's probably one of the few

people their age who doesn't have it attached to their hands at all times. "Um, I don't really have anything to change into."

I do, but it's the sweaty clothes from sitting in the heat watching Isaac play ball. There's no way in hell I'm putting those back on. I'm sure they smell horrible after sitting in the car all day.

"You don't have to worry about that." He runs a hand through his dark hair, and I don't miss the way his forearm flexes. "It's pretty low-key. Devin is out of town and she does this from time to time so it's not so lonely in that big ass house they got." He must see the indecision on my face because he adds, "you don't have to go."

"I'll think about it." And I will. Is it inconvenient? Yes. I live an hour away, and if I drink anything, I'm not going to drive home.

"Sounds good." He nods and leaves the back of the bar to finish whatever tasks he needs to complete.

Picking up the rag, I wipe down my area again before continuing down the rest of the bar. It's probably already been cleaned by Eric, but I need something to do to work through my thoughts. On the one hand, it would be nice to hang out without worrying about my kids. They are at their dad's house. If I go home, the only thing I'll do is watch whatever pops up on TV, and sleep.

If I go to Lisa's, I'll be able to see my coworkers outside of work hours. Maybe I'll make more friends while I'm there. I glance up after finishing my task and notice Eric's eyes on me. He can probably tell I'm working through my decision, and my cheeks feel hot at his stare.

It would be nice to see Eric in his natural state. When he's not trying to make the customer swoon to drive up his tips. It'll give me some insight into who he really is, and if I should take any advances, he makes on me, seriously.

Screw it. Tonight, could be a horrible decision, but I'll deal with whatever the fallout is tomorrow.

5

eric

THE BAR IS CLOSED UP, and everyone is getting in their cars. I'm always the last to leave the parking lot. As one of the managers, I take pride in making sure all of my employees get to their cars safely. Every single one of them has pulled away...except for Joan.

I lean against my car for a few moments, waiting to see what she's going to do. Still, she sits in the car. She hasn't turned it on yet. A small part of me wishes the illumination of the dash light was on her face so I can figure out what she's thinking.

Screw it. I make my way toward her car, doing my best to stay visible so she doesn't think I'm creeping up on her. And because I don't want to scare the shit out of her. My knuckles are inches from the window, ready to tap to get her attention when she opens the car door, forcing me back.

"Crap. Sorry." She closes her car door behind her.

"No worries. I wanted to make sure you were okay since

you didn't pull out of the lot when everyone else did." I nod my head to the empty lot behind me.

"Yeah, I'm fine." She runs a hand through her almost black hair, "sorry to make you wait on me."

She chews on her bottom lip. Her eyes on anything but me. "Joan," I reach out to touch her arm and think better of it, pulling my hand back. "Are you sure everything is okay? I promise whatever you say doesn't leave the parking lot."

"This is so dumb," she groans and finally her eyes meet mine. "I decided before we locked up to go to Lisa's. But when I got in the car, I realized I don't know where she lives." She throws her hands up, "and, I'll probably be the oldest person there."

A chuckle rumbles in my chest. Those are the things she's worried about. Her eyebrows furrow at my reaction. "The first thing, I can definitely help you with. You can follow me over there." I planned on going home to change, but I doubt that would make her feel comfortable. "The second, I doubt you'll be the oldest one there. I think Carlos and his girlfriend will drop by. And who cares if you are? Nobody is going to judge that." I shrug my shoulders like that's a given. "All of us are like family."

She grins, and I know she's about to have some smartass comment. "Oh really? I didn't realize family flirted with each other."

And there it is. "Okay, not like that. I mean as in we always have each other's backs." I shove my hands in my pocket, "besides, you're the only one I flirt with."

A quick glance away, and I know I've hit a nerve. Maybe I shouldn't have said that. "Are you sure it's okay if I come?" A complete change of subject. Huh, interesting.

"Positive." I take a few steps back. "Let me see your phone."

"Why?"

"So, I can put in the address in case I lose you." It's not possible in this town, but it'll make me feel better if I'm not her only source of getting to Lisa's house.

"Okay." Unlocking her phone, she hands it to me.

The first thing I do is open up the contacts and add my phone number. As much as I want to text myself so I have her number, I don't. I'm not a total creep. Instead of searching through the pages of apps she has on her phone, I search for the map. Opening it, I put in Lisa's address.

"If for whatever reason, you don't see me in front of you anymore, press start. It'll take you straight there."

She moves to open her car door. "I guess I'll see you there."

"Yep." I wait until she's in her car, with the door closed before I jog to my own. Once inside, I start it up, and wait until her headlights come on before putting the car in drive.

She creeps up behind me as we approach the exit to the parking lot. A few minutes ago, when I was talking to her, convincing her to join us, I wasn't nervous. Now, though? Now, I'm worried she's going to hate me outside of work. Not that she seems to be my biggest fan during work, but I digress.

I'll get to see her away from the bar counter. Away from annoying customers who hit on her. She'll be able to let her hair down and have fun. Tonight, is the night I'm going to take my shot. Figuratively and literally. If all goes well, I'll get some time with her that isn't awkward. At this point, what do I have to lose?

* * *

Cars are lined up along the driveway as I pull in. To my surprise Joan has stayed behind me the entire time. A small part of me thought she'd turn around and go home. Luckily, she decided to live a little...for tonight, anyway.

I park behind a car about halfway down the driveway, and turn my car off. Normally this wouldn't be a big deal, but her and Devin have a long drive, and she said this was going to be a small thing. My fingers are crossed it isn't too much for Joan.

Her car comes to a stop behind me, but she makes no move to turn off the headlights. Or her car for that matter. The lights shine brightly in the rearview mirror, and I lift a hand to block it and attempt to see what she's doing back there. Maybe she's waiting for me to get out before she makes her final decision.

I lift the handle and push open my door. I'm nothing if not a leader. Once I'm out, the sound of her engine dies and the lights flick off. Darkness surrounds me as I make my way to her.

Would opening her door for her be a bold move? I don't want to make her feel uncomfortable. She doesn't emerge after a minute, and I take that as my cue. I lift the door handle and pull it open. "Are you going to hide in the car all night?"

"I'm thinking about it," she sighs and glances at the line of cars in front of us. "I thought this was a small get together." She points in front of us, "this looks like a full-on party."

Fear and worry cross her face in a split second. "She either invited a few more people, or her boyfriend is home a day early." I hold my hand out, patiently waiting for her to accept it. "You don't have to worry about anything. Lisa doesn't let her parties get wild. If anything, she'll kick everyone out in a couple of hours. She's not the nicest when she hasn't had a solid night of sleep."

Her head tilts from side to side. I'm pretty sure she's arguing her options in her head. I don't blame her. She doesn't really know anyone here outside of work. Finally, she slips her hand in mine and allows me to help her out of her car. "Okay."

The word is almost a whisper. A soft encouragement to herself that she can do this, and I can't help but wonder how long it's been since she's gone out and done something just for her. "You can go home if this is outside your comfort zone."

"No, I'm good. I can do this. It'll be nice to have a night to myself. I don't have to worry about the kids, and I won't be the loser hanging out at home with her dad." She straightens at that last statement.

"I think it's pretty cool you hang with your dad. I spend time with my mom and brother when work allows." I wait for her to close her car door before moving us in the direction of the house.

"It's less cool when you live with him." She groans at the admission. But walks beside me down the driveway.

Pulling my phone out of my pocket with my free hand, because holy shit, her hand is still clasped with mine, I turn on the flashlight. This far down the driveway there isn't anything to light our path. It's summer and I know there are various critters around. I don't want to inadvertently come up on one. Lisa needs to add some sort of lighting down here.

"It's not so bad. I was living with my mom until almost a year ago." I shrug, "it's not necessarily a bad thing."

She snorts and stops, yanking me backward. "That's easy for you to say. You're what? Twenty-two? Twenty-three? It's an entirely different thing when you're in your late thirties and have two kids."

"I'm twenty-six, actually," I pull her forward. "Besides, age and circumstance don't matter. You're doing what you have to do."

The only response I get is bugs chirping in the dark and the sound of music carried on the wind. It's growing louder the closer we get to the house.

"How do y'all live in a place that's so...quiet?"

"Technically, I don't. I live in town and there's usually some sort of road noise at all times of the day. The noise dies down the further from town you get. We're just outside of town. Where Carlos lives is even further out, and if you think this is quiet, you're in for a treat if they do any sort of party there."

"It's just not something I'm used to." She takes a deep breath and lets it out, "even though I live in the suburbs, we're still close to the highway. I can hear traffic most nights. And if not that, it's some of my dad's inconsiderate neighbors playing loud music at all hours of the night."

"That's how it was living at my mom's house." We're even closer to the house, and I don't want the easy conversation to end. I'm not sure why she's opening up so much. It could be the curtain of night falling around us, or she feels some kind of peace. "Add no privacy and I was glad to move somewhere a little less busy."

"Privacy sounds amazing." There's a wistful tone to her voice, and it kills me to hear it. I know her kids are teenagers, and that usually means a bit more alone time. Maybe they have a different dynamic than my brother and my mom. I swear he's always holed up in his room when I'm there. It's an act of war just to get him to do his chores. If he's not in his room, he's playing ball.

"You'll get that one day." We've made it to the front yard, and I turn off the light on my phone before shoving it in my pocket. "But don't worry about that tonight. This is a time to let your hair down and have fun."

She scoffs, "easy for you to say. You know everyone here better than I do."

"You can't think like that." We take the steps together. It's only then she realizes her hand is still in mine, and she gently pulls it away. I miss the contact already. "Everyone already knows you from the bar. You'll just get to talk to them without having to wait on customers."

"You're right." She nods and straightens her back. This time not in embarrassment. She's forcing bravery, and I admire her for it.

The music is loud, even though it doesn't sound like it's coming from a radio, or speaker. I notice a piece of paper taped to the front door.

Don't bother knocking. We can't hear you. Come on in.

It's written in Devin's messy scrawl, and I was right. He's home a day early. The other cars must be from his bandmates and whoever they are dating at the moment.

"You ready?"

"As I'll ever be."

I shift in front of her, grab the door handle, and turn. Hopefully she doesn't pull away from the conversation now that we're in front of people.

6

joan

MY EYES ARE GLUED on Eric as he pushes the door open. He is surprisingly easy to talk to, and I have a feeling he sees into more than just my words. I can admit to myself that he's a good-looking guy. And he's closer to thirty than not, but could I actually give in to his requests and go on a date with him? I doubt it. I can only imagine what my kids would say.

"Y'all made it!" Lisa rushes the door and throws her arms around both me and Eric, pushing us together. If only she knew we were holding hands the entire way up the driveway. It was subconscious and felt nice. It's been so long since I've had any sort of contact with anyone I found attractive. If I'm honest, I didn't want it to end. Only the prospect of what my coworkers might think caused me to pull my hand from his.

Eric pulls away from her death hug, and she pulls me to her side. "Yep, and you should probably install some lights further down the driveway. I had to use my phone to make sure we didn't come across any snakes."

"Pfft. They are more scared of you than you are of them." I'm not sure I like how nonchalantly she talks about creepy crawlies. I'm only glad we didn't come across any. "But, it's on my list of things to do. I swear, I'm always finding new things to update or add."

Eric grins, "I guess it's a good thing you have a superstar boyfriend to have someone do it for you."

"I'm perfectly capable of doing my own home repairs." Lisa crosses her arms across her chest and glares at Eric. I have a feeling this is a long running joke between them. I know they used to live together.

"If you say so," he shrugs and closes the door behind him. "I have a screwdriver size hole in the wall I still need to cover up before Carlos finds out and kills me."

"What am I killing you for?" The man in question joins us.

"Nothing," both Lisa and Eric say in unison. If you didn't know better, you'd think they were siblings. Which I guess makes sense since they seem to be best friends.

"Hmm." He purses his lips for a split second before smiling at me. "I'm glad you came, Joan. I bet a night out without kids is amazing, I know it is for me and Caroline," he points toward the opposite side of the room where his girlfriend is talking with Angie. "We don't normally do this, but things have been so busy at the bar and we all needed to blow off steam. Plus, Lisa is the only one besides Stella with a house big enough for everyone."

"Your backyard is literal acres, Carlos," Eric slaps him on the shoulder. "You have enough room, too."

"Technically that belongs to Johnny and Stella," he glances toward me, "they let us use it from time to time."

"Enough chit chat." Lisa waves the conversation away, "let's get a drink."

She drags me toward what I assume is the kitchen. Daring a quick glance back, I notice Eric's eyes on me. The spell of what we shared on the walk to the house shattered with our coworkers surrounding us.

"I don't want to drink too much," I whisper yell to be heard over the music, "I still have to drive home tonight."

"Okay," she pulls me toward the mini bar she has set up in the corner. "But if you need to stay, I have plenty of room for you. Or," she waggles her eyebrows at me, "you can always go home with Eric."

"Won't he be staying if he's drinking, too?"

She waves my question away. "Nope. He rarely drinks at these get-togethers. He prefers to stay sober so there's a designated driver should anyone need one."

That's actually pretty awesome. Most people their age would throw caution to the wind. "One or two drinks won't hurt."

"You say that now, but you haven't had my sangria." She moves to a drink dispenser and slides a plastic cup under the nozzle. She releases the toggle and red liquid fills the cup.

Fruity drinks aren't really my thing, but I'm not going to worry about that tonight. I'm here with the people I spend most of my weekends with, and it would be good to get to know them. To have friends outside of sports parents. Not many of them have the same sort of lifestyle I do, and it's hard to relate to them. The people in this room are my people. We work odd hours and know how to talk to all sorts of customers.

Lisa hands me the cup once it's almost full to the brim

and begins filling another one. Once her cup is full, she lifts it in the air. "To amazing coworkers and friends."

I tap my cup to hers and take a long drink. "Holy shit."

"Told ya," she grins.

I have a feeling I won't be driving home after drinking just this one, but it is good. We continue drinking as we make our way around the room. Patrick is off in the corner tapping away at his phone. I'm honestly shocked he's here. He usually leaves work around ten since he does the cooking and that's what time he closes down the grill.

Lisa leaves me to my own devices when her boyfriend motions her over, and I take in my surroundings. Eric was right. It's not a wild party. Everyone is mingling. Lisa's boyfriend plays his guitar off and on. I wonder if nights like tonight inspire him to write music. Carlos even seems less grumpy with Caroline around.

I feel him move behind me before he says a word. His cologne is also a dead giveaway. "You're going to regret that in the morning."

"So I've been told," I turn until I'm facing him. "Nothing for you?"

He raises his bottle of water, and gives it a small shake. "Someone has to be the responsible one."

"You are a good human." The alcohol is getting to me. It's not a bad thing. If anything, it's helping loosen me up. "What would this tiny town do without you?"

"Probably have a boring time at the bar." He laughs, "I'm ninety percent sure I'm the personality of that place."

"Hey," I playfully smack his chest and he captures my hand against his chest with his own. I take another drink. "I happen to think I have a sparkling personality."

"You aren't wrong there," he releases my hand, but taps me on the nose. "Are you having a good time?"

"Thanks to the liquid courage, I think I am." I lift my cup and realize I'm almost out. "I need a refill."

I take a few steps in the general direction of the kitchen, and stumble forward. Eric's hands go around my waist to keep me from falling. He doesn't remove them right away when I'm steady. "How about we get you some water first?"

"But it doesn't taste as good." A small part of me realizes I'm coming off as whiny. Maybe Keith was right, I really can't hold my liquor.

"I know," he removes a hand and guides me to the kitchen. "But it will make me feel better knowing you are hydrated. If not, I'll be holding your hair while you puke into the toilet."

"Gross." He isn't wrong, and suddenly my entire body is hot. It could be the alcohol, embarrassment about possibly getting sick, or the fact Eric is glued to my side. A combination of the three? I don't know, but I have the urge to get out of the house. "Does Lisa have a porch or something in the back?"

"Yeah." His eyebrows furrow, and concern is written all over his face. "Are you okay?"

"Just hot." I fan my face to emphasize the point. Honestly, I feel like I'm sweating.

"The back porch is through these doors." He points behind him before grabbing a couple bottles of water.

He guides me to the door and cracks it open for us to slip through. It doesn't feel any cooler out here than it does inside, but the lack of people definitely helps. There's a chair to the left and he leads me toward it, but I can't make it that far. I plop on the wood deck and lie back. I didn't feel so bad when I was standing still. The second I started moving around, my stomach began churning. And it won't stop. Is it just me, or are the stars spinning?

"I don't feel so good." My hand moves to my stomach, and Eric crouches down next to me.

"Did you happen to eat anything before we came, or when we got here?"

Closing my eyes, I think back through the night. I ate some wings Patrick made me during my break. Then we got busy, and I never took another break. When we got here, Lisa pointed out the finger foods, but I never actually grabbed any. Damn it. I should know better.

"No, I didn't."

"How many drinks did you have?"

With my eyes still closed, I answer, "Two. Maybe three? I can't remember."

"Can you walk?" I can feel him leaning over me, but I'm too mortified to open my eyes and look at him. There's no reason I should have allowed myself to get like this. Especially so quickly after we got here. I'm a grown ass woman and I should be able to conduct myself better. Though, I rarely do things like this anywhere. And here I was worried about everyone else being out of control. I guess this is Karma's answer to my misgivings.

I shake my head in response, which was a bad idea. What I assume are the water bottles thud as they're set on the deck.

Moments later, Eric has one arm under my knees and he's trying to put his other arm under my back. "Joan, I need you to wrap your arms around my neck."

Can I do that with my eyes closed? I throw my arms up and hear a smack. I guess that answers that question. Slowly my eyes open and I hate how worried Eric looks. Hate even more that I'm the one causing it. I do as he says, and my arms are securely around his neck with my fingers interlocked.

He moves his other arm under my back and stands with me cradled in his arms. "Where are we going?"

"Home." His steps are slow and steady as he walks across the porch and down the steps. He can't mean my home. It's almost an hour away.

"But I don't have anything with me. And what about my car?"

"Your car will be fine." He gently shifts me to get a better hold on me. "I'll drive you over in the morning to get it."

"Okay." I lean my head on his arm, eyes pinched shut, hoping I don't puke all over him. I know I've said it many times before, but I am never drinking again.

It feels like it takes forever to get to his car, and his silence isn't helping. He's most likely using all his focus to keep from moving me around too much. Finally, he sets me on the ground, but doesn't let go as he opens the car door and helps me inside.

I want to look around his car but his body is blocking me, and I hear a click as he buckles me into the seatbelt. Then he's gone. As much as I want to snoop, I don't get the chance because the driver door opens and he slides inside. It doesn't matter anyway. My eyelids are already sliding closed again. "Thank you for taking care of me."

"It's not a problem." He turns the ignition and the car hums to life, "just rest until we get to my house."

"Okay," I murmur. "You're such a nice guy, and attractive. Too bad you're so much younger than me, I can see myself dating you."

The last thing I hear is him chuckle beside me. "I hope like hell you remember saying that in the morning."

7

eric

JOAN IS sound asleep when we pull into my driveway. She wasn't kidding when I overheard her tell Lisa she was a lightweight. But I also don't think she realized just how strong my best friend makes her drinks. Thank God she doesn't make them like that at the bar. Otherwise, we would lose money on liquor.

I put the car in park and get out as quietly as possible. I don't want to do anything to disturb Joan.

Rounding the car, I open the passenger door. I do everything I can not to wake her. Even though I know she'll feel it in the morning, she looks so peaceful.

Leaning over her, I unlatch the seat belt and let it fall into position. I grab her in my arms and pull her out of the car. It's a bit of a struggle. Lifting her off Lisa's porch was easier since there was more room to move around. The car doesn't exactly provide a lot of space.

She doesn't wake up or freak out or anything like that.

In fact, she does the opposite and snuggles deeper into my chest. This is a scenario I've dreamed about since she started working at the bar, and it's finally a reality. I would only prefer she was sober and not drunk.

Once I have a firm grasp on her, I kick the car door shut and head to my front door.

Thank God Lisa talked me into upgrading to a lock with a pin code. I don't have to mess with jostling my keys while trying to keep a grip on Joan. It's the best investment I've ever made.

Swinging the door open, the only light shining is the one above the stove. It stays on so I can see when I get home late at night.

Now to figure out where to put Joan. There's the couch, but it isn't exactly comfortable. There's also the crappy bed Lisa bought when she lived here. I don't exactly want to put her in there, either. I will take that bed and she can have mine.

I push the door closed before heading down the hall to my bedroom. I'll come back and lock the door once I know she's settled. Luckily, I didn't make the bed this morning and it'll be easier to tuck her in.

Setting her on the bed, I remove my arms from around her body. The thought of changing her clothes and putting some of mine on her passes through my mind. But I knock it away just as quickly. She can't be comfortable in the clothes she's been in all day,

I lift the blankets until she's completely covered. She may not be comfy, but she will be snug.

The bed moves as I slide off it to lock the door and get her some water in case she wakes up, but a hand clamps on my arm. "Don't go."

What do I do here? The smart thing would be to move her hand and leave the room anyway. I've never been accused of making great decisions.

Patting her arm, until she moves her hand, I get off the bed and kick off my shoes. My feet move toward the other side of the bed at an agonizing pace even though my heart feels like it's going to beat right out of my chest.

"Eric?" Joan's voice is a soft whisper in the stillness of my room.

I don't bother taking my pants off, I don't want her to wake up and freak out. She may have the idea of me being a playboy in her head, but I would never allow someone to think I took advantage of them.

I lie down next to her, on top of the blankets, and rub her back. "I'm right here."

"Okay." She scoots closer to me, and I wish this was an ordinary night. One where we end up at my place after a date. But this is fine.

Pulling my phone out of my pocket, I open the app for my door lock and engage it. Seriously, I love this damn lock.

My eyes are focused on the ceiling, even though the room is pitch black. Her soft snores fill the space between us, and despite trying to stay awake to make sure she doesn't need anything...my eyes drift shut.

* * *

Something slams into my chest. It takes me a second to realize I'm not on my usual side of the bed. And...I'm still in the clothes I wore last night. The shrieking woman next to me reminds me of last night's events, and I glance in her direction.

"Where am I?" Joan lifts the blankets.

"Do you remember anything about last night?" I slide off the bed to ease her fears.

"Not really," she scrunches her eyebrows and curls her fingers into a fist. "I know the drinks Lisa made were strong. I vaguely remember getting in the car with you." Her eyes bounce back and forth around the room. "Wait."

"Yeah?"

"You and I—" she motions between the two of us, "we didn't do anything, did we?"

"No," I shake my head. I figured she'd understand that when she realized she still had her clothes on, and I'm fully dressed. "I'm not an asshole."

"I-I'm sorry," she covers her face with her hands. "I don't think you are. It's just jarring waking up next to you."

I take a few steps toward her, but stop when she glances in my direction, and I stop. "I tried going to the guest bedroom, but you asked me to stay." Shrugging my shoulders, I slip my hands into my pockets, unsure of what to do with them. "So, I did."

"Oh." Her eyes move away from me, and I wish I knew what she was thinking.

"Are you hungry?"

"What?" The way her eyebrows scrunch together in confusion is adorable.

"You probably need food after the drinks last night," I pause for a second, "unless you don't think your stomach can handle it. Then I can take you back to Lisa's to get your car."

She pushes the blanket back and slides off the bed. Her hands brush over her clothes to straighten them out before turning to me. "I didn't know you could cook."

"There's a lot of things you don't know about me," I wink and head toward the door. I hope like hell she follows me. My steps are slow as I open the door and wait for the sound of her feet along the hardwood to let me know she's coming. Little does she know Patrick teaches me how to cook before shifts, and after staff meetings. It's one way I can impress women. Mom worked too much to really teach me how to do more than the basics.

Please let there be enough eggs to cook for both of us. Since Lisa moved out, I only have to cook for myself and the fridge isn't as well stocked as it used to be. Joan follows me through the hall, then into the kitchen. A chair slides across the floor as I continue toward the fridge.

"Do you know where my phone is?" Her voice startles me and I almost drop the carton of eggs in my hand.

"It may have fallen out of your pocket in the bed." I honestly don't remember seeing her phone last night when we left. There's a good chance she left it at Lisa's house.

She leaves the room to look for it, and I pull out everything I'll need for breakfast. I set the temperature on the oven and set two skillets on the stovetop. One for the bacon and the other for eggs. It feels nice having someone else to cook for. I'll do dinner at my mom's occasionally, but my brother is so freaking picky it's hard for me to come up with things we all like.

"It's not in there," Joan is standing in front of the counter, chewing on a nail. "I guess I left it at Lisa's." Another glance around the room to see if maybe it's in here somewhere. "Can I use your phone? I'm sure my dad has been calling nonstop."

Pulling it out of my back pocket, I unlock the screen before handing it over and turn my focus back on the food. "There isn't a ton of battery left, but it should be enough."

"Thanks." I expect her to go back into the room for some privacy, but she doesn't. She's back at the table and sitting in the chair she vacated minutes before. Even more surprising, she has the phone on speaker. Maybe she's more comfortable around me than I realized.

I look over my shoulder to see what she's doing as she's waiting for whoever she's calling to pick up. Her eyes are moving over the house, taking in everything, or lack of things, I have on display. Lisa's right, I need to add more decor in here. I try taking it in from a visitor's perspective and it looks like it's not lived in. Yeah, that needs to change.

"Hello," a gruff voice finally answers.

"Hey, Dad."

"Bug? Is that you? What phone are you calling from?"

"A, uh, friend's."

I tune out the rest of the conversation and fry the bacon while adding biscuits to a sheet pan. I didn't miss the pause before she said friend and I can only hope that means she's willing to give me a chance. That's the way I'm taking it, anyway. And what kind of a nickname is bug?

The grease pops and hits my arm, pulling me out of my thoughts. Absent-mindedly, I run on the spot and flip it. Rule one of cooking bacon, according to Patrick, don't take your eyes off the bacon. It will attack unwarranted and hurt like hell. This is why I usually cook one thing then the other, ending up in one item always being cooler than the rest.

"Do you need any help?"

I didn't even register that she was off the phone. I really need to start paying more attention to my surroundings, especially when she's around. "No, I think I have it."

"It doesn't look like it."

She's not wrong. The bacon is kicking my ass. It's not the brand I usually buy, and seems to want to torture me.

"Fine." I point to the block of biscuits still sitting on the pan. "Can you finish putting those on the pan?"

"Sure thing."

"So...Bug?" I need to know why he called her that.

"I really hoped you weren't listening in."

"Then you probably shouldn't have been on speaker." I bump into her with my shoulder. It's the most contact we've had since she woke up. I won't mention the way she curled around me as she fell asleep last night. It might freak her out.

"You're right." She takes a deep breath as she lays the biscuits a few inches apart from each other. I do my best to focus on the bacon and not her. I have a feeling I'm going to get popped again.

"So, what gives? It's not a nickname I've heard before."

"He's called me Bug since I was little. He's a fan of puns." I can almost feel her roll her eyes as she says it. "He thought my name was close enough to June bug that he said it and it stuck. I told him if he wanted to call me that, he and my mom should have named me June and not Joan."

"I take it he didn't listen."

"Nope," she shakes her head, "honestly, I feel like I should be offended he nicknamed me after a creepy brown beetle that dive bombs into everything."

"Maybe you should live up to that name." The words are out before I can stop them.

"What do you mean?"

"Well, June bugs tend to dive into things without fear. Hell, half the time without knowing what they are going toward. Maybe you should veer toward that life philosophy. You know, dive bomb into going on a date with me."

There, I took a shot, and I swear if she turns me down this time, I'll back off. Her hands stop placing the biscuits and she doesn't say anything. Fuck, I've just ruined everything.

8

joan

DID he really just use a bug as an analogy? He's not entirely wrong. I use extreme caution in my life. If I hadn't needed money for Isaac's baseball stuff, I never would have gotten into bartending. It's probably the most spontaneous thing I've done in my entire life.

"Just...forget I said anything." The oven beeps and he moves the pan from in front of me and slides it into the oven. He removes the bacon from the skillet and sets it on a paper towel covered plate.

"No, it's fine, really." Going on a date with him wouldn't be horrible. Not that I ever thought it would. It's the age thing that keeps tripping me up. I can't help but wonder what my kids would say if they knew I was thinking about dating someone so much younger than me. If I tell them. I always had a plan for when I decided to date again. They wouldn't meet him until I thought it was something more than just fun.

And he did take care of me last night. He could have

done so many things. Let me drive home, leave me at Lisa's, or just not care. He didn't, though. He brought me to his house and made sure I was safe. Hell, he's cooking me breakfast right now before taking me back to my car.

"No, I'm sorry. I shouldn't have said anything." He shrugs his shoulders as he breaks eggs into a bowl. "I just thought maybe you'd see a date with me from a different perspective."

Every time I'm determined to say no, or that he's too young, he has to say things like this. Really makes it hard for me to keep coming up with excuses not to take him up on his offer. Besides, it's not like he's asking me to be his girl-friend. It's just one date. It could be fun. I've spent so long living for my kids, and last night was a blast. Well, except for the getting drunk off my ass part and having to be carried out. I remember that part. At least he did it outside, where nobody could see me.

"What would a date with you entail?" This information is important. I definitely don't want to be hitting the clubs or anything like that. It's not my jam, and I get enough of people at the bar when I'm working.

"That depends." He pours the eggs he stirred together into the skillet he's added butter to. "What do you like to do?"

The answer should come to me quickly, but it doesn't. It's not something I've thought about in years. "I, um, actu-ally don't know."

"Have you ever ridden horses?"

"Have you?"

"No," he laughs, "but Angie's brother has a ranch and I'm sure they wouldn't mind teaching us."

"I'd have to think about that."

"We could go to the park, museums, waterpark. The

sky's the limit. There's actually a little carnival the town puts on every year. We could do that."

He convinced me last night would be fun, and it was. Maybe I'll leave it up to him. "One date." I hold up my finger and scoot back when he raises his hands above his head in victory. "Don't get too excited. I never said it's going to be more than that."

"All I need is one," he winks and goes back to stirring the eggs. "When do you want to do this date?"

He seems a bit more confident than he did a few minutes ago. His whole demeanor changed. I'm not sure if it's because I agreed to go on a date with him, or because I didn't act like an ass when he made the comment about the June bugs. Either way, I'm glad he's in a good mood.

"I'm not sure. The kids come home tomorrow." I wish I had my phone with me to see what days they have stuff going on. "And all-day Saturday is baseball. Then they are home with me until next weekend when they go to their dad's after the games."

"So that leaves tonight, or two weeks from now."

"Pretty much." This is the part I was worried about with dating. I watch Eric scoop the eggs out of the pan into a bowl and turn off the burner. The timer goes off for the biscuits, and he pulls a towel off the counter before grabbing them out of the oven.

"Breakfast is served." He makes a small bow and waves his hand toward the stove almost hitting the hot skillet he just set down. "I'll grab the butter and jelly out of the fridge. Can you grab the plates? They are in the cabinet next to you."

"Sure." Turning toward the cabinet, I open to find an array of mismatched dishes. It's cute and reminds me of when Keith and I had Isaac. We didn't have the money for a matching set, so it was whatever we found on sale or at estate sales.

After he sets everything on the table, I join him with the plates. "Crap, I forgot forks. Give me two seconds." He jogs the short distance to the drawers and grabs two forks and a knife before heading back to the table. "So, would you be opposed to going on that date tonight?"

Would I? No. But I hear my bed calling me. "Actually, I kind of want to stay in tonight and binge watch some of my favorite shows. I don't get complete silence too often." Please don't be upset about that.

"That's cool. We can wait until the next time. It gives me some time to plan." He rubs his hands together before digging into the food.

"Should I be worried?" The amount of glee in his voice feels like he's going to do something extra when I really don't need that.

"Naw." His grin is wide and I know he's going to do something more than what he needs to. "And that actually works out because I need to go see my mom tonight."

"Are y'all close?"

"Definitely. She's raised me and my brother on her own since he was a toddler." He takes another bite. It's nice seeing this downplayed version of him. The one that isn't flirting with all the customers to increase his tips.

"She sounds like an amazing woman."

"She is. I have to pick up the schedule for when I need to take my brother to his sports camps. I plan on bringing takeout so she doesn't have to cook. It's something I try to do a few times a month, even if she gets mad about it."

Hearing how Eric is with his mom, especially a single mom, makes me hope my kids turn out as caring as he has.

His phone dings on the table, and I glance at it before he can grab it. Lisa's name flashes across the screen.

"I guess she wants me to come get my car?" We need to, but I also don't want this little bubble of intimacy to burst. Getting to know him outside of the bar is refreshing. He's nothing like I imagined.

He slides open the message and reads it aloud. "Did Joan leave her phone here? I found one on the porch. I also found her car in the driveway. Please tell me you didn't take her home and have your way with her when she was drunk."

He sets his phone down and shakes his head. "What is it with y'all thinking I would stoop that low?" He runs a hand through his dark brown hair. "You, I can understand. You barely know me. But Lisa? That feels like a betrayal."

"She was probably just playing." I feel bad for assuming the worst from him. Based on his behavior at work, I should have known he wouldn't do anything like that. He always makes sure everyone is in their car before he leaves. He really is a standup guy. The only reason I even questioned it is because I didn't wake up in my normal surroundings, and my recollection of what happened last night is patchy at best.

"That doesn't make it sting any less." He scoops up another bite of his eggs, but he doesn't have the same enthusiasm from a few minutes ago.

"Then you should tell her," I point my fork at him. "She's your best friend, right?" He nods in answer. "Which is even more reason you should be able to be open and honest with her about how her statement made you feel."

"Why do I feel like you give this advice to your kids all the time?"

"I do, but it's also a good life lesson. My ex-husband

and I held so much stuff back when we were together and so much could have been avoided had we been honest about our feelings."

He stays quiet for a moment, seeming to gather his thoughts. Finally, he sets his fork down, "Would you still be together if y'all had talked things through?"

"Oh, God, no." I can't help the snort that comes out. That's embarrassing. "We probably would have gotten a divorce sooner."

He leans back in his chair. "You realize that makes zero sense."

I set my fork down, scoot back the chair, and stand. Gathering our plates, I move toward the kitchen. "True, but we were both going through the motions, pretending to be happy. Both of us were miserable and decided we were better off apart."

"That makes a bit more sense." I glance back at him and he's staring off into an empty space. I wonder where his thoughts have taken him, and if it's anything to do with his own upbringing.

"Do you want me to scrape what's leftover in the trash, or do you have a disposal?"

He jumps out of his chair and rushes in my direction. "You don't have to do that." He pulls the plates out of my hands. "You're a guest and shouldn't be cleaning up any of this."

"I seem to remember waking up in your bed, safe and sound, because you took care of me when I couldn't take care of myself." I tap my chin as if the memory is foggy and didn't happen a whole hour ago.

"Despite what people think, I'm a gentleman." He bows as he sets the dishes in the sink.

My hands reach out for a hug, but I pull back. I don't

think we're quite at the hugging stage yet. Even if he did cradle me in his arms as he carried me to his car. "Do you, um, have an extra toothbrush I can use?"

There. A change of subject to hide any awkwardness he may have seen.

His shoulders deflate the tiniest bit. I guess he noticed my gesture after all. "Yeah, if you look in the second drawer in the guest bathroom, there should be some in there. I always keep the ones the dentist gives me even though it's not the kind I like."

"Smart."

"It helps when people come over unprepared. I have a strict no driving rule when people are drinking at my house." He sighs and leads me down the hall toward the bathroom. "I've seen too many lose their lives to stupidity. It's also why I cut people off at the bar, even if they get pissed at me."

There's no way he's this good of a guy. I mean, my ex was a good guy but he wasn't a saint. What the hell kind of trauma did Eric go through to be so cautious of those around him.

"That's sound advice." Maybe he's just seen the news stories of people being over-served and horrible things happening as a result.

"I'll go get ready while you're brushing your teeth," he points at the drawer holding the toothbrush. "Then we can get your car, and phone."

Well, so much for the small talk. It took me all of two seconds to ruin whatever it was that passed between us in the kitchen. At least I have that date to look forward to. Unless, of course he's second guessing that as well.

9

eric

THE ROADS ARE PRACTICALLY empty as we make our way to Lisa's house. Most people are at church, or sleeping off last night's fun. Joan is sitting in the passenger seat, watching the scenery pass by. I honestly don't know if she's seen the town in the daylight. At least not all of it.

"Where do they hold this carnival you were talking about?" She asks as with her eyes glued to the window. "There doesn't seem to be much space to have it."

"Well, they shut down the street two streets over from the bar. But they shut down multiple streets in the downtown area." I point out a few of them as we pass them. "There's an empty lot to the side where they put a lot of the bigger rides, and then the barricaded roads hold the smaller attractions and vendors. It's seriously the best time to get fair food without having to go to the fair."

"I love fair food," her voice is soft and wistful. "I haven't been to the fair in ages. The kids get off for school, but I usually have to work and can't take them."

"Then it's settled." I slide my arm on the console until it brushes against hers. "We're going to the carnival. The fair isn't for a couple of months, and this happens to take place at the same time you don't have the kids."

Her shoulders relax, and I wonder why she had so much tension. Did she think pulling away from the hug she was initiating would make me not want to date her? That's completely absurd, but I don't know how to bring it up.

"How is that a surprise?" She glances over at me with a smirk. "I don't know what we're doing."

"Don't worry, I might have a few things up my sleeve."

"I'll take your word for it." She notices we're already leaving the town limits and getting closer to Lisa's house. "It seemed to take a lot longer last night when I was following you here."

"I was going slow. I didn't want to lose you and have you turn around before you gave us small town folks a chance."

"Excuse me." Out of the corner of my eye I can see her hand over her chest, as if she's offended. "Just because I live in the city doesn't mean I look at people in a small town any differently. You'd be surprised to know I happen to like the vibe here. It's much different than home."

"I bet." I chuckle and turn up the radio. It's loud enough to be heard, but not so loud we can't talk. "I mean, we barely have five red lights. Half the town still uses stop signs for traffic control. Oh, and all the major stores are on the central strip in town."

"You could always sit in traffic for twenty minutes to get to the grocery store."

"No thank you." Pressing on the brakes I slow and pull into Lisa's driveway. "Do you want to grab your car now and follow me to the house?"

"Shit." I think that might be the first time I've ever heard her cuss. It reminds me of Dylan's friends trying, and failing, to keep their language on a PG level for the kids. "I don't even know where my keys are."

"Open the glove box." I point toward it. "I threw them in there when they fell out of your pocket getting into the car last night."

"You are a lifesaver." She does as I say, and scoops the keys out of the compartment. I come to a stop beside her car. She opens the door and hot air flows into the car. "I'll meet you at the porch."

"Want me to wait?"

"I think I can make it to the front of the house without a guide." She laughs as she turns to close the door. "I mean the driveway leads straight to the front porch. It's not that hard to miss."

"Okay, I'll see you there."

She closes the door behind her and gets into her car. I take glances in the rearview mirror to make sure she gets in. In two weeks, I have a date with this woman, and I can't believe she actually agreed to it. I was certain after everything, she'd run screaming.

I drive the rest of the way to Lisa's house, and put the car in park. The front door opens before I'm even out of my car. Lisa leans against the door frame, Devin right behind her.

"Look who finally showed up," she taps the imaginary watch on her wrist. "I sent the text forever ago."

"Yeah, I know." Is this the moment I should bring up how her text made me feel, or do I wait for Joan to pull up. "We were eating breakfast when it came through."

"So, there were fun times?" She grins and moves her eyebrows up and down.

Yep. I need to say something now, before Joan pulls up. "Actually, no. And the text you sent was pretty crappy."

"I was just playing." She doesn't sound bitchy about being called out. More like a child not knowing the best way to approach the situation.

"Shockingly, that's what Joan said. But please just don't. I know I give off the illusion I'm a player, but if anyone knows better than that it should be you."

"I'm sorry." She holds up a hand with three fingers together. I think it's some sort of scout salute. "I won't make stupid jokes like that again."

Joan pulls up and stops the moment from getting awkward and like a scene from one of those shows that served as after school specials. She gets out of the car and makes her way up to the porch. "So, what did I miss?"

"Not much." Lisa shrugs and pushes the door open wider, forcing her boyfriend to take a couple of steps back. "Y'all want to come in? Or just stay on the porch twiddling your fingers."

A quick glance toward Joan and she already has a foot over the threshold. Well, that answers that question. I follow her in and shut the door behind me. It's weird being invited inside formally. I guess she wants to make a good impression on Joan. Usually when I come over, I barely have time to knock before she, or Devin, is yelling "come in" from somewhere in the house.

"Woah, that's a lot of food." Joan points at the kitchen counter where Lisa leads us. "We literally just ate."

"I know that now," my friend side eyes me, "but you can take some of this home. I won't be able to eat it all on my own, since Devin leaves for another tour date in a couple of days."

She doesn't give us a chance to refuse the food before she loads up plates with food before covering them.

I turn toward Devin, the guy I had to make sure was good for her when she apparently moved back into town. Something I learned when she came to work for Carlos and Angie...again. "I didn't know you had to go back out."

"Yeah," Devin shrugs his shoulders, "Crooked Halo picked up a couple more dates on the tour. We could always bow out for another act to replace us, but it's worth it for us to go out with them. It's only a few more dates, then we're home for a while."

"You're not gonna know what to do with him home all the time." I wink at Lisa and point my thumb at Devin. "But I'm sure y'all will figure it out."

"I'm sure we will." She moves closer to him and runs her hand down his back. Gross. I love them both, but I don't want to see all the cuddly stuff. I've seen more than I care to admit.

"Is it hard being away from each other for long periods of time?" Joan asks as she picks up a mini sandwich. A part of me wonders why she's asking. Is it because she's wondering how we would make dating work? Or is she genuinely curious? I hate that I don't know her well enough to know the difference.

"There's ups and downs. I think it would be easier if it didn't happen right after we got back together," she sighs. "But it's an amazing opportunity for him, and I want nothing but the best for him and the band. They've worked so hard for so many years, and I want them to succeed." She moves her hand to grip Devin's. "If that means being apart for a minute, so be it. At least there are video calls."

"Y'all are the cutest." Joan takes a bite of the sandwich

and grins. "Oh, will you be back in time for the town carnival?" She nods toward Devin.

"How...do you know about that?" Lisa cocks her head to the side, and doesn't give Devin a chance to answer. She acts confused, but I think she may know exactly what's going on.

She points toward me. "Eric told me about it," she pauses, lifts the sandwich to her lips and pulls it away. "He's, um, taking me there for a date."

"So, you finally caved?" My best friend grins.

"Let's just say he was pretty convincing over breakfast this morning." She glances at me and her cheeks redden. "With that, I think it's time I should go home. I need to get ready for work tomorrow."

"You can't just rush off after blurting that out." Lisa puts her hands on her hips. "I need details."

"You'll get those when I get them." Joan glances at me. "Do you have my phone? I really need to get home. I'm sure my dad is freaking out even though I'm a grown woman."

I can see indecision go to war in Lisa's eyes. The debate on whether or not to hold Joan's phone for ransom. "Fine." She turns around, grabs the phone from somewhere beside the fridge and hands it to Joan. "But I expect a call later."

"You'll get one." Joan waves her off and starts toward the door. At least her and Lisa get along great. I mean they were friends first, but it's been an issue with women I've dated before. They didn't like my relationship with Lisa, even though she has a boyfriend and I'm not remotely interested in her.

She pauses, and I follow after her. "I'm going to walk her out. I'll be right back."

"Yes, you will." Lisa stares at me, daring me to not come back.

I open the door and motion for her to go ahead of me. Once we're both on the porch and the door is shut behind us. I move my hand closer to hers. To my surprise she grabs it and we take the steps down toward her car. "I didn't expect you to say anything to anyone."

She loosens her hold on my hand and stops. "Was I not supposed to?"

Mere hours ago, I got her to agree to a date with me, and now I'm making her second guess herself. Stop. Saying. Stupid. Shit. Hmm. Maybe I should get that tattooed on myself to remember.

"No, it's fine," I squeeze her hand for reassurance. "I only thought you'd want to keep things quiet in case it didn't work out."

"Well, I mean people are going to see us there. It's not like Asheville is a huge city where we can melt into the crowd." She moves her feet toward her car again. "Besides, Lisa is both of our friends. If anyone is going to be dragged into the middle of whatever this is between us, it's her. Besides, we'll have to deal with all of it anyway if things don't work out. I'm not quitting the bar. The tips are too good."

She has a point. Dammit. No wonder people always tell you not to date where you work. But it's okay. I'm not going to doom us before we've even had a chance to get started. "That makes sense."

We're in front of her car and she opens the door without getting in. "Even though I woke up with a massive hangover, I had a good time today. Thank you for that."

"Well, I couldn't exactly let you suffer now, could I?"

"You are just full of surprises." She leans up on her toes and gives me a quick peck on the cheek. "I'll text you when I get home."

My hand instinctively goes to my cheek where her lips just were. She slides into the car and drives away. She's also full of surprises.

"You've got some explaining to do." I turn around and Lisa is staring at me and the look demands answers. Sometimes having her as a best friend is a pain in the ass.

10

joan

THE GIDDINESS that flows through me every time I get a text, or call, from Eric is almost ridiculous. I haven't felt this way since me and my ex first started dating all those years ago. A small string of fear passes through my gut. What if I feel all those things, only to realize we make better friends like I did with Keith?

What makes it even more weird is the fact we still haven't had a single date. That doesn't happen until next weekend, and I'm already freaking out over what to wear. I don't have any close girlfriends, aside from Lisa. I may need to get her advice because I can't ask my kids. There's no way in hell they need to know I'm going on a date. They won't hear anything about him until it progresses past that. Because in the end, my children have to like and accept him as well.

Quit overthinking. It's something I have to remind myself of anytime I get into this spiral. My brain goes from zero to ninety, coming up with all sorts of scenarios before they've happened.

"Mom," Isaac taps my arm, "are you okay?"

"Yeah, I'm fine." I glance over at him, "why?"

"You went from smiling to frowning over and over again." He shrugs and turns his attention back to the movie we're watching. Abby is hiding in her room on the phone with her friends because she doesn't like action movies.

"No, I'm good. Just thinking about things."

"If my baseball is too expensive, I can quit. I'm sure I'll still get some scholarship opportunities through my school team."

With those words, my heart breaks. It's not something he should be thinking about. "You don't have to worry about that. I've actually made enough tips at the bar that it's covered this season and I've put some back for during the year if you aren't playing other sports."

Most people wouldn't talk about money with their children. Hell, I don't most of the time, but it's good to be honest. If anything, maybe my kids will always have those open conversations if they decide to have families of their own. I can't help but feel like a hypocrite at the same time. If I were being truly honest, I'd tell them about my date with Eric, but I'm not ready for that yet. Uncertainty at how they would react, or judgment they may pass at being with someone other than their dad, eats away at me.

"I haven't decided yet."

"Huh?"

He laughs. "Sports. I don't know if I'm going to play the school ones in the fall. It depends how I'm feeling once it's closer to the school year."

"That makes sense," I nod in agreement as a bomb goes off in the movie. "Just know I'll support whatever you choose to do. And I can take care of baseball if you want to play in the fall."

"Thanks, Mom." He leans his head against my shoulder, reminding me of all the times he did this as a child. I mean, he's still a kid, but he's as tall as me, and I don't get these small moments anymore. Not since he became a teenager and thinks he doesn't need his mom anymore.

The only thing that would make this moment complete is if Abby would come out of her room and hang out with us. Not that I mind. I should schedule more one on one time with each of them.

The movie is winding down and I move the popcorn bowl to the coffee table. "Do you have any plans for the weekend after the game?"

"I was actually going to ask..." he trails off and doesn't say anything else.

"Ask what?"

"If a couple of my friends can stay over after the games?"

This is the part I hate about working on the weekends, especially working late. "You'll have to talk to Grandpa. You know I don't get home until really late. If he's okay with it, then I'm fine."

"I'm sure he'll be okay with it."

"Just a couple of friends, Isaac," I narrow my eyes at him. "Not the entire team. I know Grandpa thinks he's still super young, but he isn't. And no offense, but y'all can be a lot."

Rolling his eyes, he shakes his head. "My whole team isn't half as bad as Abby and her friends."

"Be nice to your sister. She's not even here to defend herself."

"Says who?" Abby says from the hall entry. "At least we

don't annoy the crap out of you when they spend the night."

I can already tell this is going to turn into a battle. Holding my hands up between them, I give a pointed look at each of them. "Let's not do this tonight. It would be great if y'all could go one day without fighting."

Abby tilts her head to the side, debating how she wants to proceed. Sighing, she nods. "Okay, Mom. Sorry." She sits on the other side of me on the sofa, and leans her head against my shoulder. She only ever does this when she wants something.

"What do you want?"

"Who says I want anything?" She looks up at me and bats her eyes. Good grief she's laying it on thick.

"Spill." I nudge her with my elbow and she sits up. "Might as well get all of the asks out at once."

"Well, if money is included in that ask, can I have a hundred bucks?" The sly grin crossing her face lets me know she's not being serious. Before I can say anything, she continues on with her requests. "Since Isaac has friends staying the night over here, can I stay the night at Chloe's?"

It's better than them both having friends over for the night. I'm not sure my dad could handle all that despite what he thinks. "Yeah, that's fine. As long as it's fine with her parents."

"I wouldn't have asked if it wasn't."

"You don't have to have an attitude." Isaac pipes in.

My daughter's only response is an eye roll. Most days I wonder if I'm capable of raising two teenagers at the same time. Both kids have mood shifts at random times, and while I'd like to think they'll talk to me when something is going on...there are days when I think they don't. I'll be patient, though.

"How are you getting there?"

She loses all of her mood and looks at me. "Her parents can get me. They know you work nights."

A small part of me wonders if they know I bartend, and if they judge me for it. I don't have the luxury of giving it much thought, though. I have to be able to take care of my kids and make sure their sports are paid for.

"Okay," I grab the popcorn bowl off the table and stand, "are you going to the games with me on Saturday?"

"No." She shakes her head, "they are going to get me around lunch. I think we may be going skating or something."

"That's fine." One less stop I have to make. This time I'll make sure I have a bag ready to change into for work. "I'll leave some money for you before we head out. Just call me when you get to where you're going."

"I will." It feels weird telling her this two-days before she plans on going, but she'll be asleep when I leave tomorrow and it looks like I won't see her again until Sunday. "Love you, Mom." She rushes over to me and gives me a quick hug before retreating back to her room. Those are the moments I live for.

Isaac gets up and gives me a quick hug. "I'll see you bright and early Saturday morning unless I'm still awake when you get home tomorrow night."

"You better not be."

He shrugs. "Night, Mom."

Now it's only me standing awkwardly in the living room holding a popcorn bowl. I wonder if this is how most parents find themselves at the end of the day.

* * *

"Do you own sunscreen?" Lisa asks me from her section of the bar.

"Yeah, why?" I covered my entire face before leaving for Isaac's games this morning. There's no way I should have a sunburn.

She moves toward me and boops the tip of my nose. "Because you're in here looking like a certain reindeer," she gives me a quick hug. "How are you gonna impress the guys if you're all red?"

"I'm not trying to impress anyone." That's a lie. I know it as soon as the words come out of my mouth. Lisa knows it, too. She shakes her head and moves on to a customer.

"I guess it's a good thing I've seen you at a pretty low spot, huh?" Eric walks by me. "Though, I'm pretty fucking impressed by you every day."

He's laying it on pretty thick. "If you say so."

Out of the Ashes is probably the most fun place I've ever worked, but everyone here is so nosy. It's not just the staff either. Customers have been glancing between me and Eric since I got in. For a crowded bar they are paying way too much attention to me, and I don't know how I feel about it.

The same guy from last week comes up to my section, and Eric's warning flashes through my mind. I have a group of people crowding my area. He could have easily gone to one of the other two bartenders, but he chose me. The way his eyes linger on my chest doesn't exactly give me a great feeling. Maybe Eric was right. I'll have to tread carefully to keep from giving him the wrong impression.

The man waits his turn until he's directly in front of me. "How come I never see you working during the week?"

If there's one thing I've learned watching crime shows, it's you never let a person you're not sure about know your schedule. He's harmless, I'm sure, but I don't want to chance it.

Avoiding the question, I grab a rag and wipe down the counter. "What can I get you to drink?"

He gives me an order for a draft beer and leans over the bar. His elbows set halfway over the counter, putting him as close as possible to me. "Maybe on your next break, you can grab a drink with me."

That's a hard pass. What in the world gives this guy the impression that this is okay behavior. "Sorry, I can't drink while on the job."

"Yes, you can. I see him do it all the time." He points toward Eric. He's not wrong. I've seen him do it, but he's always behind the bar and usually at the request of a woman to get higher tips. Not that he has to work hard for those. His jar is always full by the end of the night.

"It's a personal choice." There. That should shut this shit down.

"One drink." He holds one finger in the air as I slide his drink to him. I'm doing my best not to come into close contact with him. While I'd like to think he wouldn't grab my hand, I'm not completely sure. "It won't even take your full break. Besides, what will it hurt?"

He's not getting the clue. "I don't have any more breaks for the night. Sorry." I shrug and smile. Another lie, but he doesn't know that. Unless...he's been watching me. I'm not sure when he came in, but from his insistence and slur of his words, he's probably been here a while.

"I don't see what the big deal is." His voice is louder this time, garnering the attention of those behind him, waiting to place their orders. You'd think one of them would step in, but they don't.

"She said no." Eric's voice booms from behind me.

When did he get over here? I've been so busy trying to gently get this customer to go that I didn't notice him.

"This isn't any of your business," the guy snarls. "Why don't you go back over there and serve drinks? We are having a conversation."

"We really aren't." I mutter under my breath, but it's apparently loud enough for the guy on the other side of the counter to hear.

"Yes, we are." He tries to reach over the bar to grab my hand, and I instinctively take a step back. Bumping into Eric before he moves in front of me.

"It's time for you to leave."

"I just bought my drink." He grabs his mug and takes a drink. "I'm not leaving until I'm finished."

"That's where you're wrong."

"What are you going to do? Make me?" The man snorts and takes another drink. "I'd like to see you try."

Eric pushes me back, preparing to launch over the counter and do just that. But someone else grabs the man by the arm. "Time to go."

I think it's Angie's boyfriend, but I can't be sure. I've only seen him a handful of the times I've worked here. Eric leans down until his eyes meet mine. "Go to the office."

There's no point arguing with him, even if I wanted to. I walk past Lisa, around the bar, and toward the hall. The crowd parts for me like the Red Sea. It's not until I reach for the door knob that I notice my hand is shaking.

11

eric

MY BLOOD IS PUMPING, itching for a fight. How dare that asshole think he can put hands on her. He's never gotten like this with any of the other bartenders. I don't know if he had too much to drink, or if he's just a dick. It doesn't matter. He's not going to treat any of my employees like he's entitled to them. Especially her.

Before I realize what I'm doing, my feet are carrying me to the end of the bar. I pause briefly by Lisa. "Can you handle this for a minute? I want to make sure he leaves, and doesn't hang around."

"Yep." She nods, "I'm sure everyone will understand."

I hate leaving her alone behind the bar on a busy Saturday night, but this is the only thing that will ease my concern. After I make sure he's gone, I can check on Joan. I push through people until I'm out the front door. Delilah is staring at me, wide-eyed.

Red and blue lights illuminate the side of the building, and I want to thank whoever called the cops. We haven't had issues with patrons in a long time, and I'm glad Dylan was there to handle the situation. Before he started working with Johnny, he handled any unruly people that came into the bar when it was getting popular.

A hand shoots out in front of me as I stomp down the sidewalk, and my hand lifts to hit whoever is stopping me. "It's taken care of, man."

I didn't even see Dylan leaning against the wall. "Who called them?"

"I did." He nods to the cops putting him in the back of the car. "As soon as I noticed he wasn't going to leave the new girl alone, I had a gut feeling. Sucks, I was right."

"Yeah, it does." Taking a few deep breaths, I try to calm my rage. My emotions don't typically get the best of me, but Joan didn't deserve any of that. "Are they towing his car, too?"

"I'll call someone after the bar closes so we can make sure it's his vehicle that gets towed."

"Thanks, man." I turn back toward the door. Now that I know he's taken care of, I need to make sure Joan is okay. "Can we add him to the banned list?"

I don't typically like adding people to that. Mistakes are made, but he crossed a line with Joan tonight. He could do it again.

"Already plan on it." He follows me to go inside. "He'll probably only sleep it off in a cell tonight, but Delilah is my next stop. I know I can't tend the bar, but I'll stick around to help if you need to pull one of the waitstaff to help behind the bar."

"Thanks," I open the door and step in. "Pull someone who doesn't have a lot on their hands. I need to go check on Joan."

"You got it."

Weaving through the crowd doesn't take too long. They must see I'm in no mood to deal with foolishness. My steps slow as I near the door to the office. I don't know what to expect when I step through, but she needs someone to make sure she's okay.

I knock three times on the door to let her know someone is coming in. "Yeah." Her voice is shaky, and hard to hear over the music pumping through the speakers.

Slowly, I turn the knob and push the door open. "Hey, Joan. Are you o—" She rushes into my arms before I finish the question. Her arms go around my waist and she leans her head against my chest. I close the door behind me and move out of the way in case Dylan comes in.

"I'm sorry I didn't listen to you before."

With one arm around her shoulders, I use my free hand to smooth down her hair. Trying to think of how else I can comfort her.

"It's okay. You didn't know."

"But you did. I thought I could handle myself with anyone. He was so persistent, and wouldn't take no for an answer."

"You did fine." I pull her closer to me, hoping like hell she's okay with it. She doesn't move away. If anything, her entire body relaxes into me.

"Is he still here?"

"No. He'll spend the night in jail until he sobers up." I rub her back. "He's also banned from the bar."

"I didn't mean for you to lose a customer."

"He was an asshole so don't think any more of it." He's also not the first person we've banned. Most of the time people who act like that have been kicked out of other bars. Soon they'll have no place to go, and I'm perfectly fine with that.

We stand in this close embrace for a few moments. The music from the bar filters into the office. Her breathing slows, and I think she's coming down from the adrenaline of the interaction. She doesn't immediately pull away, and I'm glad for the comfort she finds in me.

"Sorry, I should...probably get back to work." She mutters into my shirt. She starts to pull away, but I keep her in my embrace.

"Don't even worry about that," I whisper into her hair. "Stay in here as long as you need. Or, you can go home if you want."

"No, I can't do that." This time she does pull back. Her hands sliding down until they are in mine. "I really need the hours and tips. Both kids in sports aren't exactly cheap."

"It's up to you, Joan." I rub her knuckles to keep her calm. "You'll get paid regardless of what you do."

She breathes a sigh of relief. "Thanks." She looks around the office. "I think I'll stay in here for a bit and see how I'm doing. Right now, I don't think I could drive."

It may be selfish, but I was hoping she would stay. Even if she's not working the bar, I'll know she's here...safe. "Okay. If you need anything, come get me. I'll send Dylan back with some food."

She scoffs. "You're going to have the boss's boyfriend wait on me?" Laughing, she leans closer to me. "Something about that just seems weird."

"It's what he used to do when he worked here. I promise you he won't mind. He actually offered to pitch in so one of the waitstaff can pitch in at the bar." Actually, a better question is why is he here tonight without Angie? She probably had that book club thing all the girlfriends and wives do.

"Crap." She gasps and her fingers slip from mine. I

already miss the softness against my own. "I didn't even think about that. You need to get back out there. I'm sure Lisa is overwhelmed."

"You'd be surprised what she's capable of. I know she's sweet and nice, but that lady knows how to command a room."

"You're not lying." She shakes her head and moves toward the chair in front of Angie's desk. "Now, go. I'll be fine. If I need anything I know where to find you."

A small smile crosses her lips and I'm sure she's faking being okay so I'll go back to my job. My feet lead me to her and I crouch down until our eyes meet. My hand moves of its own volition to push a strand of hair that's fallen from her ponytail out of her face. She shivers at my touch. Is it good? Bad? I don't know.

"I'm serious, Joan. Anything you need, let me know." She opens her mouth but I cut her off, "and if you feel the need to go home early, do it."

"I will." She pushes at my shoulder, almost knocking me to the ground. "Now go."

She shoos me away and I do as she asks. I need to relieve Lisa. She may know how to hold her own, but it's a busy night. It'll be like old times where we split the bar in half.

One last glance at her as I open the door. She'll be fine. She has to be. That guy, however, better never try getting in this bar again. I can't promise I'll wait for the cops to get here.

* * *

The bar has cleared out. Well, at least the patrons have. The rest of us are cleaning up so we can get on with our nights. Or sleep. Joan didn't come out while we were still serving.

Not that I blame her. I'll be surprised if she wants to keep bartending. That sort of treatment isn't something I've really had to worry about, but I see it happen with female bartenders time and time again. It's ridiculous it has to be worried about in this day and age.

Right now, she's helping Lisa clear the tables and wipe them down. I told them I'd take care of the bar. The two of them are whispering and shooting glances my way. I wonder what they are talking about. Clearly, I'm the subject.

Throwing the dirty rag in the bucket under the bar, I round the bar. Dylan steps in front of me. This is becoming a habit. "Can I help you?"

"You don't need to go over there all nosy."

"I wasn't—"

"Yes, you were. I know you better than that." Of course, he does. That's what happens when everyone who works here is a close knit group.

"What are the chances of that guy coming back?"

"It happens, but they are going to let him know when he gets out of the tank in the morning that he isn't welcome." He snaps his fingers in annoyance, "damn, I forgot to get a picture to share with the other employees."

"I don't think you'll have to worry about that," I clap him on the arm. "We've all had run-ins with him. We just have to describe his attitude and they'll know exactly who we're talking about."

"If you say so." He shakes his head and sighs, "Angie is going to freak out when I tell her we had to ban someone."

"I'm sure she'll know before you even tell her." Snorting, I head toward the dining area to put the chairs on top of the tables. "It's like you've forgotten what town you live in."

"You're right." He follows me and stacks chairs. "Let's get this done so we can get out of here."

Patrick comes out of the kitchen with the broom and a mop bucket, and I lean toward Dylan. "Did you know he was still here?"

"Yep." He continues stacking chairs. "I have no idea why. He's usually gone by now, but I'm sure he won't tell you if you ask him."

"True." Our beloved cook is amazing, but keeps to himself most days. The only people I really see him talk to are Angie, Stella, and Carlos. Maybe it's the whole age thing. We probably feel like children to him. Even though I don't think we're that much younger.

Patrick starts sweeping and Lisa goes behind him with the mop. Where did Joan go? I hadn't heard the bell above the door, so she didn't leave.

Tap. Tap. Tap. Something hits my shoulder in quick succession. "Thanks for being there for me tonight." Joan's voice is soft, but loud enough to be heard by me alone.

"Hopefully we won't have that issue again." If anyone was paying attention tonight, they got the message about acting like an ass. This was way past strike three for that guy.

"God, I hope not." She looks up at the ceiling as if it holds all the answers. "I've never been put in that position before. I didn't know how to react. I thought if I let him down gently, he'd leave."

"You can't reason with people like that. They feel like they are entitled to everything, and refuse to take no for an answer."

"Well," she huffs, "guys like that can kiss my ass. I never want to feel like that again."

"You won't." I reach for her hand, and am surprised she

allows me to take it. Maybe she likes me more than she's willing to admit. Future date aside, and all that. "Next time anyone asks you the same question more than once, get me or one of the other guys. We'll take care of it."

"Does that offer only extend to me?"

"Nope. It goes for anyone who works here." A gentle squeeze of her hand, and her fingers interlock with mine. "We were lucky Dylan was here and called the cops before I got my hands on the jerk."

"You don't need to get into fights because of me."

"There isn't really much you can do about that." It's time to change the subject. I don't want her thinking I'm always out looking for a fight. "Are you about to head home?"

"Honestly, I don't want to yet."

"I thought you had your kids this weekend."

"I do," she rolls her eyes. "Abby is spending the night with a friend, but Isaac has a couple of teammates spending the night. I'm sure they'll still be awake when I get home. And a bunch of teenage boys isn't exactly what I want to deal with right now."

"Maybe we can have a mini date?"

"Is that even a thing?"

Patrick shoos us away as he gets closer with the broom, and I honestly forgot anyone else was here. "More like grabbing breakfast at the diner. It'll push off going home, and we can hang out."

I can see her warring over what to say. If she gives in to want or responsibility. All I can do is wait.

12

joan

HE'S STARING at me with so much hope. There should be no doubt in his mind that I'll eat with him. I literally told him I wasn't ready to go home yet.

"What if we go pick up the food and go back to your house?" He looks like he wants to argue, but I add, "I don't really want to be around people."

He chuckles and runs a hand over my arm. You'd think I would shy away after that asshole tried to grab me. I don't though. With Eric, I know I'm safe. Even if I wasn't interested in him, more than I should be, I know I'd be safe on his watch. That's the kind of guy he is. Always looking out for everyone who works here.

"I'm not sure if you know this." He leans toward me and whispers, "but I'm people, too."

He always has to be the funny guy. "You know what I mean." I pull away from him to get out of Patrick's way. It's weird he's still here. He's normally long gone. "After being around a shit ton of people here, I don't want to be around a lot of people."

"I doubt there are a lot of people at the diner. It's the middle of the night." He follows me back toward the bar area, but keeps talking. "But if that's what you want to do, your wish is my command."

Dylan and Delilah are by the bar, having what seems like an unofficial meeting as we approach them. "I swear, if people keep coming in here acting like jerks, Bryce won't want me working the night shifts." Delilah groans and leans against the counter.

"I thought it doesn't happen often." At least, that's what Eric told me earlier.

"It doesn't." Both Eric and Dylan speak at the same time.

Dylan continues, "I can count on one hand how many people we've banned. Don't get me wrong, we get a couple of unruly folks every once in a while. But rarely does anyone actually try to lay hands on an employee."

"That makes me feel slightly better."

"How much longer do we need to stay?" Delilah asks Eric. I figured she would defer to Dylan since Angie is his girlfriend, but I guess he doesn't have much authority here.

"As soon as Patrick and Lisa are done, we can head out." He nods toward Dylan. "You don't have to stay."

"I know, but I need to call the tow truck for that guy's car, and I want to make sure I get the right one." He glances to the side where my fellow coworkers are putting the mop and broom away. "Y'all can head out if you want. I can lock up."

Delilah jumps at the chance. "I'll see y'all next shift." She stops by the podium and grabs her wallet and keys. Within a minute she's out the door.

Eric doesn't budge until he sees her headlights flash across the door. I'm honestly surprised he didn't walk out with her. He usually makes us walk out as a group to make sure nothing happens. Not that she gave him much of a chance. I don't blame her, though. She probably wants to spend some time with her boyfriend.

"Are we good to go?" Lisa asks as she walks out of the kitchen.

I nod before anyone else can say anything. "Dylan said he'd lock up."

"Sweet!" She does a little dance. "I can go home and get some sleep. It's weird sleeping in that big house when Devin is gone."

My mouth opens to invite her to eat with me and Eric, but at the shake of his head I close it. I move toward her and give her a hug. "Hope you get some rest. Not much longer until he's home for a while."

"Be careful going home." I don't correct her as she walks out the front door. I turn to Eric and look up. "You ready?"

"Yep." We wave bye and head outside. It's still stupid hot despite the late hour. "How do you want to do this? We can leave your car here and we can ride together. You can follow me, or I can pick up the food and meet you at my house."

"I can meet you at the house." I head toward my car and he follows behind me. Lisa gives a quick honk as she pulls out of the parking lot. "I'll just wait in the car until you get there."

"Don't be ridiculous. I'll text you the code so you can get inside."

"It's fi—"

"Don't bother arguing. There's no point in you sitting

in my driveway. The neighbors may call the cops if they are up to being nosy." He shrugs, "besides, it's not like I have anything to hide."

"Fine," I groan. It's going to feel weird being in his space without him. I mean, I've only been to his house once, but I didn't exactly see much to keep me occupied.

"See, arguing would have been pointless."

He leans down and gives me a peck on the cheek. I stare at him, dumbfounded. Heat replaces the spot his lips just touched. Oh my God, now is not the time to freak out. Also, how long has it been since I've let any other person be affectionate like that with me. Too long to count.

"I'm sorry," he mutters. "I shouldn't have done that without asking."

"No, it's fine." My hand instinctively moves to my face, and I force it down so I don't look like a lovestruck woman. "Do you, uh, want to text me the code?"

"Yeah." He pulls his phone out of his pocket, tapping quickly before placing it back. My phone dings in response. "What do you want to eat?"

Oh, yeah, that. It's been so long since I've had breakfast in the middle of the night. Definitely before I had kids. "How about waffles, bacon, and hash browns."

"A girl after my own heart." He places his hands on his chest for emphasis. "I'll call it in so it'll be almost ready when I get there."

He slowly backs away, eyes on me, until he bumps into his car. I wouldn't have opposed another kiss, but I know he felt bad about the peck. "I'll see you at your house."

"See you there." He waves for me to get in my car and doesn't budge until I'm safely inside and buckled in. Finally, he moves around his car until he does the same. I see him reach for his phone once more before lifting it to his ear. There's no point waiting around for him. I turn my car on and head out of the parking lot, wondering what I'm supposed to do alone in his house while I wait for him.

* * *

The quiet in the house is overwhelming while I wait for Eric to get here. I don't see a radio anywhere to listen to music, and I'm not the type to rummage through his things to see what type of person he is. That's best left for conversation.

I spy a gaming controller on his tv stand and I move closer to see what it is. It's the same one we keep in the living room at home. Mostly because it's the only one with games I know how to play. The ones Isaac plays aren't anything I can get into no matter how much I try. He always hands me a controller, but I typically die within minutes. Sometimes even seconds.

I grab the remote and controller and turn on the TV. I also press the power button on the console. The output I need lights up, and I press it. With any luck he has the games I know.

His profile pops up, and I fight the urge to click on it. Just because I'm not the type to go through his house, it doesn't mean I won't check out what games he's playing.

My finger hovers over the button before I use the joystick to select the guest profile. Hopefully I can still play whatever games he has on here.

Multiple games fill the screen. Some of them are the same ones Isaac plays, and I have a feeling they'd get along great. Well, aside from the fact that he's much younger than me, and I'm not sure my kids want to see me dating anyone else.

I move the joystick around until I find a game I absolutely love. It's a simple racing game, but it is so much fun. I loved it as a kid, and my own hate playing with me because I always beat them.

Selecting my character, I pick the tracks I want to race on. I always avoid the ones with water because it never fails. I get stuck going slow by taking too wide of a turn.

Racing cup through cup, I'm engrossed in this game. Someone clears their throat and I jump, hitting a banana peel another car has thrown into the road.

"You should probably lock the door when you're here at night alone." Eric stands by the table with a bag in his hand. "And now that I know you like to play video games, it's on."

"Shhh, I'm trying to concentrate." I've been knocked into third place and that just won't do. I hit a box and a star pops out of it. This is what will win the race for me. I hurry through the obstacles knocking people out of my way until I cross the finish line.

"Are there any other games you play?" Eric sets the containers on the kitchen table and I set the controller on the table in front of me. He doesn't bring up the incident at the bar, and I'm grateful. It's not something I want to dwell on.

"Not really," I stand to join him. "Isaac keeps trying to get me to play the zombie games with him, but they take me out almost as soon as I get started. I'm more old school."

Gah, that makes me sound ancient.

"There's nothing wrong with that." He slides a chair out for me to sit. "All these games have become popular again. I remember Patrick trying to get that tiny console that has all the games on it so he wouldn't have to buy a gaming console and individual games. Come to think of it, I actually don't know if he ever got it."

I know exactly what he's talking about. I begged Keith to find one for me, but they were sold out at all the stores. The only place he could find them was an online site, and they were marked up for way more than they are worth.

Shrugging, I sit down in the chair as he pulls orange juice out of the fridge. Grabbing two glasses he joins me at the table. "You can't mess with the classics."

"True." He opens our containers and hands me the silverware they included. "Do you play often?"

"Not really." There's not enough time in the day for me to enjoy myself. It's one of the reasons I'm protective of my Sundays. It's the one day I don't have to do anything. Well, besides get everyone ready for the next week and wash all the laundry accumulated over the week. "By the time I get home from my other job, it's time for dinner then running the kids around to various practices. And the weekends are pretty much booked with games and work."

"I guess that means we'll be gaming over here every once in a while."

"You act like you're going to get more chances at a date with me after next weekend."

He points his fork at me and grins. "You act like you're not."

Wow. Someone is cocky tonight. Right now, though, I can't really deny that. The more time I spend with him away from everyone else, the more I want to get to know him.

"So, does tonight count as a date?"

"Nope."

"Why not?"

"Because we aren't going out anywhere. Yes, I bought

dinner. Or would it be a super early breakfast?" He tilts his head to the side. "It doesn't matter. But technically I haven't taken you out. Therefore, it's not a date."

"You realize that doesn't make any sense. It's perfectly fine to hang out at either of our houses, preferably yours, and call it a date."

"Why mine?" He seems genuinely curious.

But how do I explain I don't want to introduce him to my kids if we're only going to date a few times. Hell, how do I know he won't find me boring and move on to someone else?

Someone his age that has the freedom to do things without having to work around a schedule with kids. It really isn't fair to him. I take a few bites of my food to gather my thoughts.

"Because..." I don't get a chance to finish because my phone dings with a message.

There's only three people who would be texting me. I pull my phone out of my back pocket and open up the screen.

Isaac: Where are you? You're usually home by now.

Of course, he's still awake. No doubt wondering if I can grab some late-night tacos for him and his friends. Unless, of course, he always stays up until I get home and I don't know it.

Joan: I'll be home soon.

Isaac: can you get some tacos...

Joan: Let me know how many.

Eric's eyes are on me when I look up from my phone. "Sorry, I have to go."

"One of the kids? Is everything okay?" His eyebrows knit in concern.

"Yeah, my son noticed I wasn't home yet and asked where I was."

"I get it." He does, and I know he does. But it doesn't stop the slump in his shoulders when I scoot my chair back.

"Thank you for super early breakfast."

"Anytime." He walks me to the door, opening it, and following me to my car. "Sorry you couldn't finish it."

"That's the way it goes with kids sometimes." I unlock my car, but I don't want to leave him like this.

I move my arms around his neck and lean up on my toes. My lips meet his, and I can taste the syrup from the waffles. It's sweet, and the exact opposite of how I'm feeling right now.

His arms go around my waist, and he pulls me closer, deepening the kiss. His tongue moves across mine, and I melt into him. I want to do this the rest of the night.

My phone dings again, and I pull away.

"To be continued." Eric leans down and kisses me one more time.

"Next weekend I'm all yours."

"I'm counting on it." He opens my car door and waits until I'm inside before closing it.

I turn on the car and pull out of the driveway. This time I don't stop my hand from lifting to my lips as I drive away.

13

eric

JOAN'S abrupt departure is still running through my mind and it's been a couple of days. I understand she has kids, probably better than most men since I'm the product of a single mom. But they are also teens. Surely, they could get by long enough for her to finish her food.

"Eric," Mom's voice cuts into my thoughts. "Are you listening to me?"

Normally she'd be at work today but decided to take the day off to take care of some stuff for the little brother. Hopefully she's also taking care of herself. At least I bought us lunch.

"Sorry, Mom." I take a bite of the burger to the sound of a video game in the background. Cameron should be in here. We're trying to go over the rest of his practice schedule and going over the games we know about when the school year starts. The only way Mom can plan her schedule is if we know which sports he's going to play. "My mind is somewhere else."

"Is it a girl?" My mom nudges my arm and when I glance at her, she's grinning. "Actually, don't answer that. I know it is. I haven't seen that look on your face since you dated that girl in high school you thought you were going to spend forever with."

I'm not sure how I feel about her calling me out like that. Also, the leap to thinking it will be forever is also not what's happening. It can't. "We haven't even gone on our first date yet."

"When is that happening?"

"This weekend." Do I want to tell her my plans? She has a way of being too nosy for her own good and might try to take matters into her own hands. Screw it. She may actually have some advice for me on how to navigate these murky waters with her. "I'm taking her to the fair in Asheville. Then maybe dinner. It depends on what she wants to do."

"That sounds fun." She takes a few moments to eat some fries before she asks me more questions. I can see the wheels spinning in her head. Maybe I should have lied and not said anything at all. "Tell me about her. What's she like? How did you meet her?"

The TV in the living room gets louder, and I know my brother is trying to drown out our conversation. He just wants to make sure we aren't talking about him. He's only nosy up to a point. It's something both of us get from our mom. It's good, though. I don't need him trying to orchestrate anything either. Huh, now that I think about it. I'm exactly the same way. Look at how much I pushed my friends at the bar to go after their relationships. Maybe I'm more like my mom than I thought.

Now where to start. "She's older than me."

"How much older?"

"I don't know exactly. She has two teenage kids around Cameron's age."

My mom's mouth drops. Maybe I should have started off with the fact we work together. To my shock she doesn't actually say anything horrible. "Oh, well. Dating a single mom comes with its own hurdles. Different circumstances that can make things tricky."

"Yeah, that's something I'm starting to realize. She works at the bar with me on the weekends. I know she does it for extra money for her kids playing sports."

"I know that struggle." She's contemplated getting a second job so many times. Things are more expensive than they were when I was in school, and Cameron's sports are no exception. "I already admire her for that."

"I just don't know how to handle this. She ate a late dinner with me last weekend after we got off work, but didn't get to finish because her son texted her asking her where she was. She left right after the text."

Mom rests her hand on my arm, pulling my attention away from my food. "I'm going to tell you now. It'll be hard. Her kids will always come first. At least until she knows if the two of you are going to be serious." She takes a deep breath, "she has to guard her heart and make the right choice when it comes to dating. But it's not just her heart she has to protect. She has two others that will be impacted. That's not an easy thing to decide. Why do you think you never met anyone I dated?"

Wait, what. "I didn't know you even dated anyone."

"I'm just like every other human on the planet. I get lonely, too," she sighs, "it just never worked out with anyone because they didn't want my baggage."

It's kind of gross the men she dated referred to us as that. I think it may also be an area where I have some expertise because my mom did raise us alone. "I'm glad you never brought those douchebags to meet us then."

"And that is why you have to be patient with her."

She has a point I've never considered before. Like, I knew things with me and Joan wouldn't move as quickly as it has with girls prior to her. But I didn't realize her feelings would be on such a deeper level.

"I'll do my best to be patient." I take a bite of my food and think for a moment. "So, I shouldn't push to meet her kids."

Mom slaps my arm and I flinch. "Not if you know what's good for you. Let her lead that discussion and be prepared for it not to happen."

"Well, that doesn't bode well for me," I grunt.

"That's why you don't need to go falling head over heels for this woman just yet. Put your guard up until you know it's the real deal."

It may be too late for that. The protectiveness I feel for her is the same as it is for those I love, and we haven't even gone on one date. I'm falling for her as the person she is. Honestly, that's enough for me.

"I'll do my best."

"Good. Now let's get your brother in here."

He takes his time coming to the table after she calls him. Her phone and calendar, that's usually on the wall, placed in front of her. It's like she pulled it out of nowhere. I guess it's time to do what I came over here for, figuring out Cameron's schedule and how we are getting him to all the places.

"Do we have to do this right now?" He groans as he plops into the seat.

"Yes," Mom scolds him. "School will start before you know it, and we have to get this worked out. In case you haven't noticed your brother and I work. We have to shift our schedules and it's best to get our boss's adequate notice."

"I guess." He rolls his eyes and slouches over the table.

Mom and him are arguing back and forth. It's like watching a ping pong match. I tune them out and count down the days until I can see Joan. Our date on Sunday needs to go off without a hitch.

* * *

I wish Joan could spend the weekend in Asheville, even if it's not with me. Work tonight was busy, but we didn't have the drama of last weekend. That guy hasn't made an appearance since then, and it's been a relief. Well, I say he hasn't. There's no way of knowing since he wouldn't make it past the stand and I barely see that depending on what area of the bar I'm working.

"Wanna grab a late dinner?" My steps coincide with Joan's as we approach her car. Everyone else has already left. Aside from Patrick. He's leaning against his car while checking his phone. I can't help but wonder what exactly he's avoiding. It's not like he lives with anyone.

"I should probably get home." She lifts her arms and pulls her ponytail tighter. "Isaac will be wondering where I am, and we have an early morning tomorrow."

'Another long day of baseball before you come into work, huh?"

"That's putting it mildly." She laughs and stops beside the driver door. "He has three games, and I'm not prepared for the sun beating down on me."

"I can always join you." The offer is half jest and half

serious. "You know you need someone to hold an umbrella over to keep you from getting a sunburn."

She giggles and shakes her head. "As tempting as that sounds, I'm not ready to explain whatever this is between us."

Not exactly the response I wanted. Even though I know what my mom said about letting her lead that discussion, I can't help it. The pull I feel to be around her is frustrating. With all the dates I've been on with women the past couple of years, none of them hold a candle to the intrigue she has.

"Okay." I don't know what else to say to that. "It'll give me more time to plan our date on Sunday, and dinner for tomorrow night." I pause for a second. "You're staying with me, right?"

She lifts a hand and places it on my arm, soothing away her previous rejection. "Who else would I stay with? I don't exactly know very many people here."

"There's always Lisa," I shrug. "Or even Stella, or Angie. There are always options."

Taking a step closer to me, she puts both of her arms around me and looks up. "Lisa, I could understand. But the other two...we're acquaintances. We haven't really worked our way up to friends."

"Understandable." I wrap my arms around her. "I can make the bed in the spare bedroom for you. Do you need me to get anything special for you while you're here?"

"Or you could not do that."

"So, you're going to sleep with me in my bed?"

"Don't get too excited." She pokes me in the rib and I flinch. "Just because we'll be sharing a bed doesn't mean anything is going to happen."

"Hey, I never said it was." Doesn't mean I'm not going

to prepare for it. I'd rather have protection than not have it. There aren't many stores that stay open twenty-four hours in town. I'd have to go to the bigger town, and that's a buzzkill.

"And, I don't need you to get anything. I'll bring everything I need."

"Okay. Just wanted to make things easier for you."

"I know," she leans her head against my chest, "and I'm sorry if I upset you about coming to the games tomorrow. We haven't even gone on our first official date, yet. Meeting my kids may scare you off, and I don't want to rush you meeting them."

"I get it." Damn my mom for being right. One of these days I'll actually listen to her and not do whatever the hell I want. "My mom actually warned me about that. It was this whole discussion on when she was dating, and I didn't even know she was."

Joan jerks her head back. "Y—you told your mom about me?"

"I didn't really have to." Rolling my eyes, I continue, "apparently I was rocking the lovesick look and she guessed."

"Hmm."

What does that even mean? Is it a good noise? Bad? Further proof I'm completely out of my element when it comes to Joan. Here I am, thinking I'll be the perfect person for her to date since I come from a single mom household. But really, I know jack shit about how to tread these waters.

"She told me to be patient. So don't worry, she's not planning our wedding or anything."

"That's good to know," she grins and leans up on her toes. "I like you, but I'm not ready to think about the distant future."

"Me either." I pull an arm away from her and lift her chin until her eyes meet mine. "I'm more focused on right now."

"Same." Her voice is breathy.

Both of us meet in the middle and our lips meld together. This is why I wish she was staying tonight, too. I'm addicted to the way her lips taste. To the rush I feel even with only kissing her. If I feel this intense about something so PG, I can't imagine how it's going to feel when I get to have her completely. Not that it's happening this weekend or even in the next couple of weeks. That's another area I'm perfectly fine with her leading. Pushing her too hard about things she's not ready to do will only result in me losing any chances I have with her.

I deepen the kiss, tongue swirling with hers, and move my hand to the back of her head. My fingers tangling in her hair. It'd be easier if she didn't have it up, but that's fine. Pulling her closer to me, her body flush with mine, she tightens her hold on me.

A ringing comes from out of nowhere. She pulls away, and I glance to where Patrick was parked. He's long gone. I didn't even notice his lights when he left. Or hear his truck. It's as if the entire world falls away when I'm with Joan.

It's not my phone because it stays on silent until I get home. Joan pulls hers out of her pockets and groans.

"Kids?" I ask, even though I know the answer. It's like they have a sixth sense. Twice now they've called while we were kissing.

"Sorry." She silences the phone and slides it back into her pocket. "I don't understand why Isaac has started checking up on me."

"I'd do the same to my mom if I were in his shoes." I

can't begrudge the kid for wanting to make sure his mom is safe. But damn, his timing sucks.

"I guess. It's just weird. He's never cared before."

"Have you always worked late into the night far from home?"

"Not really. My weekday job is about twenty minutes from the house."

"Don't hold it against him. He's a teenager and wants to be the protector. I get it."

She gives me a quick peck on the cheek. "I should probably go before he starts blowing up my phone."

"Text me when you get home?"

"Yeah." One more kiss and a hug before she gets in her car. I watch her drive away, and hope like hell our date this weekend goes uninterrupted.

14

joan

THE KIDS ARE GETTING ready to head out to the game for the day, and I'm staring at the contents on my bed wondering what the hell to pack. I can't believe I'm willingly staying at Eric's tonight. Last time it was a fluke because I was too inebriated to drive home. This time...is different. We're going to spend time together and go on a date. It's been way too long since I've done any of this. Over my head doesn't begin to cover what I'm feeling.

"Mom," Abby yells from the living room. "Are you almost ready?"

Crap. Time to go already? Luckily there's no need to sneak a bag out of the house. They suggested I take one after finding out I didn't have anything to change into after the last game.

No time to decide now. I scoop up the clothes on my bed and shove them in the duffel bag. It's fuller than usual, but hopefully they don't notice. The last thing I need, or want, to do is explain myself to my kids. If things work out, I'll fill them in. Until then...this is a bit of fun for me.

My door slams open, Abby standing in the middle. "Are you coming?"

"Yep. Sorry I had to get my bag ready."

She eyes the bag as I lift it on my shoulder and smirks. Perhaps she pays more attention to me than I thought she did. She's usually holed away in her room on the phone with her friends.

"Grandpa and Isaac already left." She rolls her eyes, "he wants to get there earlier than he needs to be to practice more."

Sounds about right. No matter what Isaac always does what he can to be the best on the field. It doesn't matter that he hasn't played as long as some of the other kids. He's determined.

"Why are you wanting to leave so early? The first game doesn't start for at least forty-five minutes."

"I'm hoping we can stop and get donuts."

"That's not exactly fair to your brother."

"He does the same thing all the time when we're at Dad's. Besides, if I eat it on the way, he'll never know." She raises her eyebrows up and down, conspiratorially. She is too much.

"Okay, but if he finds out, it was your idea."

"I'm okay with that." She walks toward the door, motioning for me to follow her.

Damn, she's not even giving me a moment to myself. I hope like hell I have everything. If not, I'll be making an early morning run to the nearest store.

Within twenty minutes we have donuts and are on the way to the ball fields. We're stopped at a red light and I take a drink of my water. "So, who's the guy?"

Water covers every surface in front of me. Glancing down, I notice the wet spot on my shorts. Great. It's going to look like I peed myself.

I cannot believe she just asked that. There was no anger or resentment, only curiosity. And, she had to wait until I took a drink to ask. It was most likely on purpose. "Who says there's a guy?"

She sighs, and shakes her head, clearly annoyed with me now. "Mom, my brother may not see the clues, but I have. You're in a much better mood. And, you've been doing your makeup more than you ever used to."

She's not wrong. The makeup isn't to impress Eric, though. It's because I feel happy and when I'm happy, I wear makeup more often. Especially the brighter eyeshadows.

"Would you be upset if there was?" Everything I do tonight hinges on her answer. The light turns green, and I let off the brake. A silent prayer she won't ask me to ditch the only other person besides them and Dad who brings me joy.

She sits in silence for a moment, thinking through her answer. Her favorite pop singer plays low on the speakers. Finally, she speaks and places a hand on top of mine. The action is shocking, and my heart melts at the sincerity.

"Not really. At least, not right now. My brother is a different story, but I say follow your happiness. You're an adult, and you're allowed to see people."

This generation of kids is going to change the world. The empathy they have to situations is astounding. Isaac will be a harder sell, but it's not like I'm itching to introduce Eric to them yet.

"That means a lot, Abby." I take a deep breath. At least this conversation is over with one kid. "If that changes, promise you'll tell me. You and your brother come first."

She nods her agreement. "I'll let you know when we meet him. If he gives off a bad vibe, you'll be the first to know. So, where did you meet him?"

Her body shifts until she's turned slightly toward me. One foot under her leg. Her reaction will tell me exactly how she feels.

"He actually works at the bar with me." That was vague enough. I leave out the part where he's younger than me, and technically my boss.

"Oh, that's cool. So, you get to see him all the time."

"Well, yeah, when I'm working. He's taking me on a date tomorrow."

"Is that why you have a bag? Are you staying the night with him?" That's a little bold, and that part is none of her business.

"I always have a bag. I don't want to go to work in sweaty clothes."

"I know, but your bag seems...fuller." So much for my hope that she didn't analyze it too much when she saw it on my bed.

"It is because I'm staying in Asheville tonight." I turn on the blinker to turn into the sports complex. "I don't want to mention him too much because who knows if things will work out between us. I don't want to muddy the waters within our family until it's a sure thing."

A quick glance her way and she's staring out the window, deep in thought. Good, she's going to let the subject drop.

"That makes sense." She pauses for one second. Two. "Just give us a heads up if we're going to meet him."

"Of course," I shake my head. "I wouldn't spring that

on you and your brother. What kind of person would that make me? I do respect the both of you."

"I know. It's only to ease my mind."

"Understandable." A person close to the field Isaac is playing on pulls out of their spot, and I take my opportunity to pull in. "Now, let's watch your brother kick some butt before I have to go to work and y'all go to your dad's."

* * *

One day we'll be slow on a Saturday night, and I won't be exhausted. Tonight is not that night. With the fair being set up and running, we had all sorts of people come in after being in the sun most of the day. I even had to park at the back area of the lot instead of close to the door like I normally do.

All of us are dragging our feet while going through our cleaning routine. Even Carlos and Angie came in to help out with orders. Patrick stayed way later than he normally does. Definitely an all hands-on deck situation.

"Are we almost done?" Lisa groans as she pushes the broom around the floor. Honestly, I'm not sure how much she's actually sweeping compared to the time she takes to lean against the closest wall.

"I hope so." Various coworkers call out at the same time. I swear sometimes it's like working with a hive mind. Most days I feel like I'll never fit in because I only work with them two days a week. It feels like a family and I'm on the outside waiting to become part of it.

"Y'all get out of here," Carlos waves us on from the hallway. "Me and Angie will finish up. No staff meeting in the morning. Enjoy the fair while it's in town."

"Yes!" Lisa flings the broom handle to the side and does

a dance I'm pretty sure I've seen on one of Isaac's video games. She's my closest friend here, but there are times the difference of age is apparent.

I grab the dish cloth from my hand and move toward Carlos. "Are you sure you don't need us to stay longer? I feel bad y'all are doing this just the two of you."

"Yeah, I'm sure. The rest of you got a lot done, it won't take us long to finish up."

"If you're sure..."

"I am," he glances over at Eric. "Have fun tonight, and maybe we'll see you at the fair tomorrow."

"Does everyone know?"

"Pretty much," he shrugs and pulls the cloth from my hand. "If I don't run into you tomorrow, I'll see you next weekend."

Wow. So much for keeping things low key until we know we mesh well together. Though apparently everyone we work with thinks it's a done deal. There really are no secrets when it comes to this bar.

Turning toward the bar area, I search under the cabinet until I find my wallet and keys. It was so packed when I got here that I didn't bother taking it to the office.

"Are you ready to go?" Eric leans over the countertop making no secret he's checking me out while I'm bent over.

"Yeah, I think so." My knee pops as I stand up and I hope he didn't hear it. This whole getting older business sucks.

"Want to meet me at my place while I pick up food?"

The idea of eating isn't even appealing. Right now, all I want is a pillow and bed. I'm not normally this tired but between the crowd tonight and the sun earlier today, my eyes may not stay open very long.

"Actually, can we just go to your place? I'm good with a bowl of cereal or whatever you have there."

"Are you feeling okay?" He tilts his head to the side, studying me.

"Yeah, just tired. It's been a long day." I move until I'm standing beside him. "And I need some rest if you're going to show me all the wonders of this fair y'all have."

"Don't mock it just yet." He grabs my hand and leads me to the front door. Everyone is filing out in front of us, and finally we get to leave for the night. "We may be a small town, but we do put on a pretty awesome shindig."

"Can't wait to see it." He walks me to my car, and opens the door for me after I unlock it.

"Are you okay to drive?" Bending down his eyes meet mine, making sure I'm not going to fall asleep while driving.

"Yes. Your house is like five minutes away. I'll be fine." I duck down into the car to avoid his worry. Childish? Maybe. But I'm not going to pass out in such a short drive.

"Okay. Give me a few minutes to make sure everyone gets out of the lot. Then we can head to the house."

A quick nod to acknowledge my agreement. We will definitely need to have a talk about him being so overprotective. This level of tired is nothing like the sleepless nights I had with the kids when they were babies.

He's standing in front of my car with his arms folded across his chest, watching every car as they leave. It's good to know that protection doesn't just cover me. He truly cares about everyone we work with. A part of me wonders if something happened to his mom, or someone he knows, to want to make sure any of the women who work at the bar get in their cars safely.

It's also something I didn't think people would have to

worry about in a small town. In the city for sure, I've been approached by some not-so-great people walking to my car at the grocery store. But I guess a person can never be too safe. Just look at the guy who tried to manhandle me in a crowded bar. The audacity of people is unparalleled.

Finally, the last car leaves and Eric turns to give me a thumbs up before climbing into his car. As exhausted as I am, I'm nervous. Tonight, I'll be sleeping in bed with another man, totally conscious of my actions this time around. I haven't slept with anyone other than my kids or ex in years. God, I hope I don't snore. Time will tell, and tomorrow morning I'll wake up mortified or everything will be amazing.

15

eric

IT'S HAPPENING! Joan is staying the night with me. On purpose this time. I spent all morning deep cleaning. Not that my house is dirty in general, but I need to put my best foot forward.

We pull up to my house, I stop at the curb so she can park in the driveway. I'm unbuckled and out of the truck before she has the car in park. My front yard is small and it takes no time to cross it to open the door for her.

"Do you have a bag?"

"It's, uh, in the backseat." She moves toward the back door, but I block her attempt.

"I got it." Opening the door, I pull the strap of the duffel bag toward me. Damn, what does she have in here? It feels pretty heavy for one night.

"And that's why I was going to get it." She laughs and closes the door behind me.

Our hands slip together and we walk side by side to the front door. Moving my hand from the shoulder strap of the bag, I put in the code and swing the door open. "I'm going to put this in the room. I think I have cereal and I know there's stuff for sandwiches."

"Okay." Her hand slips away from mine and I already miss the contact. Not that it matters tonight she'll be right beside me. "I'll make us some sandwiches."

"Sounds good." I head toward the room and put her bag on top of the dresser. My eyes bounce to every area of the room to make sure it's perfect. I don't smell that thing my mom got me, though. I check the plug only to find the device on the floor. Well, crap. One day I'll remember to plug things back in after using the vacuum.

Pushing the device into the outlet, I move the dial to make more of the scent fill the room, and call it good. The bed is perfectly made and the pillows I never normally use are arranged in a tidy row. Honestly, I don't see the point of the throw pillows, but every woman I know has them covering their bed.

I pull the door closed behind me as I head toward the kitchen. Joan's phone is on the counter and there's a voice-mail playing on speaker. "Hey June Bug, I know you're at work and this is your kid free weekend. I just wanted to see when you're going to be home so I can make plans of my own. Call or text me when you get this. Love you and be careful."

She makes a face at the phone. "What plans are you making, old man?" It's not like he can answer her. But I wonder if her mind is going down the hole of wondering if he's also dating. It's valid. I go through that thought process when Mom asks if Cameron can stay with me overnight. Now I know she's definitely going on dates after our talk the other day.

My assumption is that she's only spending one night,

but maybe her dad knows more information than me. "So, are you going to text him?"

She jumps at the sound of my voice. "You scared the crap out of me."

"Sorry."

"Yeah. I was actually going to wait and see how tomorrow goes before I asked if it was okay if I stayed tomorrow night as well. I mean, I can go home, but I wasn't sure what time we'd be done with the fair. I brought extra clothes just in case so I can go straight to my weekday job." She shakes her head and sighs, "sorry, I'm rambling."

"It's okay." I grin and round the counter. "On both fronts. Even if tomorrow is a disaster, you can sleep in the guest room. I'm really not the type to hold grudges."

Not saying it won't hurt, but that's a bridge I'll cross if we get there. The peanut butter and jelly are sitting on the counter, and I glance down at the sandwiches she's making. "Except maybe now. What on earth are you doing?"

She lifts the slices of bread in the air. "Making sandwiches."

"No, you can't make it like that. Peanut butter only goes on one side of the sandwich, not both."

"You're wrong." She sets them down and proceeds to pick up the butter knife to spread the peanut butter on each slice of bread. She sets that down and picks up the jelly, squeezing a decent amount on one of the pieces of bread. Lifting another knife to spread it evenly, before setting the pieces of bread on top of each other. "You need it on both sides to make it a stable sandwich. Otherwise, you get jelly all over your fingers as the bread softens."

"But that's so much peanut butter!" This is ludicrous. I've been making pb&j sandwiches my entire life, and not once have I had an issue. Sometimes jelly seeps through the bread, but not enough to make me change the way I make my sandwiches. "And it's not how I learned to make them."

"Well," she shrugs her shoulders. "You learned wrong. Just hold all judgment until you try it this way."

"Fine." She hands me one of the sandwiches. We should go to the table to eat, but I want to prove my point. The sandwich does feel more secure. I'm not telling her that, though.

Lifting the sandwich to my mouth, I take a bite. The blob of peanut butter I expected to take over my mouth isn't what happens. The peanut butter is spread thinly enough that it's not overwhelming, and I don't look like a dog trying to eat it from a spoon. It's honestly the perfect ratio of peanut butter to jelly. Damn it. She's right.

"So, what do you think?" She leans against the counter, watching me. The self-satisfied smirk tells me she knows exactly what I'm thinking.

"It's okay." I will not bow down quietly. Mostly because I want to see if I can recreate it exactly the same. These are my go-to snacks when I get home from work, or a jog.

"Hmm." Her lips spread into a wide smile. Yeah, I'm not fooling her. She quickly eats her sandwich and starts putting things away. "Is it okay if I take a shower before bed? I feel disgusting."

"Sure." I brush off the crumbs on my hand into the sink. "The bathroom is in the hall. There should be towels and anything you need in there."

"Thanks." She leans up and kisses my cheek. "I won't be long."

My feet almost follow her into the bedroom while she gets her things. But it's okay for her to have space in my house. I have nothing to hide. Except maybe the box of condoms that sit in the nightstand drawer. I wasn't playing about being prepared. You know, just in case.

Grabbing a paper towel, I brush the crumbs on the counter into my hand before dumping them in the sink. A quick rinse later, and the kitchen is clean.

It takes a few moments for her to get her clothes, and I finally head to my room after I hear the bathroom door click shut and the water falling from the shower head. I need to get ready for bed while she's busy.

* * *

Someone needs to define the word quick. It feels like it's taking ages for Joan to get out of the shower. Or, it could be my nerves playing tricks on me. Either way I don't think I've ever been this antsy when it comes to a woman staying over. Not that it happens often. I usually went to their place because it's easier.

There's only one thing to do while I wait for her…scroll through my phone. Mostly I'm looking at the social media accounts for the fair the town puts on. It'll be nice to know what areas to make time for, and which ones we can skip.

Finally, she walks into the room. Her hair is in two braids and she's not wearing any makeup. She doesn't normally wear a ton, but I like this version of her. Relaxed and confident in herself. The shorts she's wearing however, are tight and short. They almost look like ones you'd wear when working out. She's trying to kill me.

She glances at the clock by the bed. "Oh my God. I'm so sorry, I didn't mean to take so long in the shower. How in the world is it already two in the morning."

"No worries." I chuckle. "I'm not usually asleep yet anyway." It's a lie. I usually fall asleep as soon as I get home.

She sets a bag on the floor in front of the dresser. I guess it's her dirty clothes, and turns toward the bed. "Um, what side of the bed do you want me to sleep on?"

"Doesn't matter." I stand and let her decide.

"Yeah, I don't believe that." She rolls her eyes. "Everyone has a preferred side of the bed."

"No, really. I'm okay with whatever side you want. You seemed to sleep pretty well on that side last time you were here." I wave my hand toward the side I typically sleep on.

"I was also drunk off my ass." Her head shakes. In shame? I can't tell. "But, fine, I'll sleep on this side."

She moves the comforter back and slides onto the bed before pulling it over her. I wait until she's settled to turn off the light, then I flick it back on again. "Fan or no fan?"

"Fan, please." Shit. I'm going to freeze my ass off tonight.

Leaving the switch on, I pull the string that turns the light off. It's a good thing I know my room like the back of my hand. Otherwise, I'd be fumbling in the dark, unsure of where I'm going.

It feels weird lying next to someone in my bed. Not in a bad sort of way, but in an I could get used to this way. It provides an intimacy I've never allowed.

There's movement over the comforter and for a second, I think some sort of spider is moving its way to bite one of us. But I feel Joan's fingers slip between mine. She turns to her side, pulling our joined hands over her waist, before scooting back until her body is pressed against mine.

What else am I supposed to do other than turn toward her. Our bodies fit together perfectly like puzzle pieces. She snuggles further into me. Her ass rubbing against my cock. She's definitely trying to test my willpower.

A part of me wonders if she's doing it intentionally, or

if she's the type that likes to snuggle and needs a feeling of security wrapped around her.

"So, are you staying another night?"

"I don't know." It may be dark in here, but I can hear the smile in her voice. "I'm strongly considering it. Why?"

"Just wondering." Inside I'm hoping that turns into a yes. I can definitely get used to this. Having her beside me every night. But that isn't something I can think about now. We have to get through the dating phase before that's ever a possibility. Plus, there's the logistics to think of.

Her shirt rides up the slightest bit with her movement, and I rub my thumb over the exposed skin. She shivers under my arm and I want nothing more than to flip her over and have my way with her. I won't though. Not unless she initiates it. I'm going at her pace.

"We should probably get some sleep. Tomorrow is going to be a long day."

"Yeah, it just takes me a minute."

She keeps moving around. At first, I thought it was because she wanted things to progress, but now I wonder if it's because she hasn't had someone else in bed with her in a while. The feeling is mutual. We'll work through it, though.

It takes me a while to get settled because all the plans for tomorrow run through my head. It needs to be an epic day. Every time I close my eyes to fall asleep another idea pops into my brain and then is interrupted by the crickets chirping in the summer night. Both my brain, and the insects, need to shut up already.

16

joan

IF I THOUGHT it felt weird being in Eric's house alone the first time, it's even more so now. When I finally fell asleep, I was wrapped tight in his arms. It's probably the best sleep I've gotten in ages.

This morning, though. He was nowhere to be seen. I've gone through every room in the house. No Eric. There aren't any notes on the counter or anywhere else that I can see. Who does that?

While I wait for him to show up, I take a few moments to text Dad. Honestly, I'm surprised he hasn't text me again since I didn't answer him last night.

Joan: I'm probably staying here again tonight. I'll be home after work tomorrow. What plans are you making?

Dad: Probably the same ones you're making. Have fun and don't do anything I wouldn't do.

Joan: Gross.

Dad: Love you.

Well, that confirms some thoughts I had about him

dating. I assumed he was because he hasn't been home much when I'm off work. I don't think he realizes the kids are capable of staying home by themselves. But I'm glad he cares to be there for them just in case.

The front door swings open and I jump. "You scared the hell out of me."

"Sorry."

"Where were you? I looked everywhere." There's way too much panic in my voice, but I can't help it. It's odd being in a place I don't know well, and being alone.

"I'm sorry. I go for a run every morning."

"For fun?!?" That doesn't sound like a good time to me. I know the kids go for runs when they are conditioning but they have a reason. Neither of them would just go for a run if they don't have to.

"Yeah." He laughs and takes a few steps toward me, attempting to give me a hug. I step back. He's hot and all, but he's sweaty and gross. "It helps me clear my mind."

"If you say so." Though, a small part of me wonders what exactly he had to clear his head about this morning. "What time are we leaving for the fair?"

"I have no idea." He runs a hand through his hair. "I wasn't expecting you to be awake already. I planned on getting a shower and grabbing breakfast before you got out of bed."

"We can always go out for breakfast." It seems like I'm always putting a hitch in his plans for us. I probably could have slept longer, but not feeling him next to me was worrying. "Or, I can make us breakfast."

He's already shaking his head before I get the words out. "Today is about you. If anyone is cooking, it's me."

"I'm perfectly capable—"

"I know you are," he interrupts me, "but I don't want

you lifting a finger. For once, let someone do something for you."

How does he know I typically do everything on my own? Accepting help is hard for me, and I don't think it's something I'll ever get used to. Even though my dad helps frequently, I constantly try to pay him or do things around the house to show my appreciation. I can't just leave it alone.

I'm about to ask him where he gets his insight, when I remember he was raised by a single mom. He probably knows better than anyone how much of ourselves we give those we love, especially our children.

"Fine." I sigh. Not because I'm mad, but because I don't know what to do with myself if I'm not doing something for others. "I'll let you plan out the day, including breakfast."

"Good." He nods his head to prove his point. "I'm gonna take a shower then I'm going to get breakfast for us."

"I kind of want to see your cooking skills again."

"Believe me, what you saw that one morning is about it. Mom didn't have a ton of time to show me how to cook. I watched when I could, but I mostly live off fast food, and things I can throw on the grill."

"And peanut butter and jelly sandwiches." I grin, and take a step toward him. Sweaty or not, I wrap my arms around his waist. The contact may not mean much to him, but to me, it's everything.

"Yes, those too." He pulls me closer to him. "Even if I've apparently been making them wrong my entire life."

"You said it. Not me."

He kisses the top of my head and pulls away from me. I already miss the closeness between us. The pull I feel toward him is more than I even felt for my ex-husband when we first met.

"You go back to bed, or play the video game. It doesn't matter which you do, just relax while I take a shower."

"I can do that."

"Can you?"

"Yes." It's annoying how well he seems to know me even though the only time we've spent together is the weekends we both work at the bar. "You don't need to be a smartass."

He holds his hands up in surrender. "I'm just making sure."

Without another word, he heads to the bathroom to shower and get cleaned up. Every cell in my body wants to wash the few dishes I saw in his sink, but he told me to relax.

The only way I'll accomplish that is if I go back to bed. Normally I'm not the type to go back to sleep after I've been awake for a while, but I'll try.

I hear the shower running across the hall from Eric's room. But that's not the only sound. Is he...is he signing? The words are muffled, and I can't figure out what song it is. Maybe I should ask him when he gets out. I push the thought from my head for now.

Eric's room is almost completely dark. The only light seeps through the edges of the blackout curtains, and the dim yellow from the bulb in the hallway. I should really invest in those curtains. The combination of the curtains and being in Eric's arms gave me the perfect night's rest.

My phone is sitting on the nightstand, and I glance at it to see if there are any messages. None. Hmm. I guess Abby is doing what she can to make sure Isaac doesn't blow up my phone today. It's something I'll never understand because their dad is literally in the same house, and he'll call me to settle a dispute. Make it make sense.

Pulling back the comforter, I climb back into the bed I left less than an hour ago. I know there's no way in hell I'll be able to go back to sleep, but I can enjoy the peace and quiet for a while. Something that doesn't happen often at home.

It's not long after I've laid down that the bedroom door widens. Eric walks inside in nothing but a towel. A small gasp leaves my lips, and the towel almost falls to the floor. He catches it before it can slide all the way down.

"I'm sorry. Did I wake you?" He glances around the room, unsure what to do now.

"Not at all. I was taking a moment to enjoy the solitude, and you happened to walk in."

"Is that a bad thing?" He grins. He knows exactly what he's doing. And damn it, I know it's payback for the way I was leaning into him last night. I expected him to make a move, but he didn't.

Hell, I needed him to do it. I don't know what I'm doing when it comes to sex. I mean, of course I do, I have two kids. Just...not in this new territory where I'm not with the person who fathered those kids.

Find your voice, Joan. "Not necessarily." Thank God it's dark in here because I'm certain my cheeks are now a bright shade of red. "It was just unexpected."

"I'm gonna grab some clothes and change in the other room."

"You don't have to." The words fly out of my mouth. There's no reeling them back in now. "I mean, I can always go to the living room. You shouldn't have to upend your routine because I'm in your space."

There. That should fix things. Maybe?

"Okay," he drawls. "Your comfort level is what I care about. I didn't want you running for the hills."

"Yeah, there's no chance of that happening this morning."

"Keep making comments like that, and I'll have to join you in bed." His grin is devilish. One side lifted up. His eyes glitter with mischief in the light from the hallway. He's doing his best to test my resolve.

Honestly, I'm not sure I have the willpower to deny him. Not just for him, but because for me. It's been so long since I've been intimate with anyone and I don't know where to start. Seduction hasn't been a part of my arsenal for a long time.

"Okay." The words are a whisper leaving my lips. So quiet, I don't know if he heard me.

His eyebrows lift up and his mouth drops open. He didn't think I would follow through with it. Well, jokes on him because today is about me. He said so himself.

"Ar-are you sure?"

Hell no, I'm not sure. I'm terrified. But I pull all the confidence I have front and center. The word already left my mouth. He's giving me an out, but I'm not going to take it. For the past sixteen years I've been a mom first, it's time to be a woman first. Even if things don't work out between us, I know he won't make it horrible. He's shown through every interaction we've had that he's a gentleman.

Nodding, I move over on the bed. Thanking the universe it's still mostly dark inside. I may want to be touched in the worst way, but I don't know if I'm ready for him to see me naked in the light. Motherhood hasn't exactly been kind to my body.

I'm not sure if he can see me, but seconds later he joins me. The towel is still wrapped around his waist as he slides under the comforter. He reaches for my hand and slide mine into his. "We don't have to do this if you aren't ready. I don't want you to feel like I've pressured you."

"I know. I want to."

He turns on his side, and leans on his elbow, his face hovering over mine. I can't see his expression. "You can tell me to stop at any time and I will."

"Okay." Now that he's here, next to me...I'm nervous. I haven't been celibate since I divorced Keith, but it's been a while. My body looks nothing like women his age. I've had two kids, and gravity has taken its toll in some areas. The confidence I felt moments ago is quickly slipping away.

Most of the light is blocked out by the dark curtains he has over the windows, and that makes me feel marginally better. At least he won't be able to see all of me.

"You don't have to be nervous." His free hand combs through my hair, doing his best to calm my fears.

The only way things are going to work between us is if I'm completely honest with him. Past experiences have taught me that much. "It's not that I'm nervous." I take a deep breath and let it out. How am I going to say this without sounding ridiculous? "But look at you. You're muscular, in shape, and basically any woman's dream. And I'm...not."

I shift my gaze to the opposite side of the room. I don't want to see the look of horror he likely has. Or, see him agree and get out of the bed. Both would be a punch to the gut.

His hand that was stroking my hair minutes ago moves to my chin, and he gently pulls my face toward him. He doesn't say a single word until my eyes meet his. "Whoever told you that needs to be throat punched." I open my mouth to tell him, it's me that needs it, but he doesn't give me a chance to say anything. "You are the most beautiful woman I've seen. You're also the most stubborn, but we won't talk about that."

"Hey, no I'm not."

"It took you forever to want to date me. I'd say that's pretty stubborn."

"Whatever." I roll my eyes and try to scoot away from him.

"You don't have to take my word for it. I'm going to show you just how beautiful you are."

His lips close the distance between mine, and I know I'll never be able to come back from this.

17

eric

I THOUGHT HAVING her in my bed the last time was amazing. Now...now she's in my bed and has made it certain she's interested in more than sleeping.

Her lips are soft and hesitant as mine meet hers. It kills me that she doesn't feel completely comfortable in her own body. But this morning, I intend to change that. She needs to know how beautiful and desirable, she truly is.

She shivers as I slowly run my fingers down her body. As much as I want to devour her the way I've dreamed about for weeks, I'm determined to take my time.

As I inch my way toward the hem of her sleep shorts, she hooks an arm under mine and pulls me closer. I don't want to ask her how long it's been since she's been intimate with anyone, it's not really my place, but I have a feeling it's been a while.

Scooting backward, I pull her with me until she's in the middle of the bed. The chance of one of us slipping off the edge is pretty big since this bed isn't very large. My lips never leave hers.

"Eric," she pulls away and takes a shuddery breath. "I need you."

I don't need her to ask twice, but I'm not going to give her what she wants just yet. I will, however, give her what she needs.

Moving until I'm settled between her legs, I kiss her one more time. My mouth leaves hers, and I press soft kisses along her jawline before working my way down her neck. Her shirt is still on. It's definitely a roadblock, but right now I think that's the only thing bringing her comfort. It's a security blanket, and I can't take that from her.

Moving the shirt up a few inches, I trail kisses down her stomach before sliding my hands over her waist and pulling her shorts down my mouth draws a line down her thigh. The way her whole body shudders at the contact lets me know I'm on the right path.

She moves her legs closer together, and wiggles them to push them down. Now that those are out of the way, I settle in between her thighs. Taking a few seconds to make sure she's okay, I glance up to find her eyes on me. I'm about to verbally ask her if she's good, but I don't get the chance. Her fingers slide into my hair, and she grips it, leading my mouth where she wants it to go. I'm happy to oblige.

Her thighs clench around me as I taste her. Soft moans pour from her lips, and warmth floods through me. I'm the one making her whimper. Her fingers tighten in my hair as she comes apart, and holy shit is it intense. I'm not even inside her yet, and I'm so close to coming.

Joan's breathing evens out and I move until I'm hovering over her. Reaching out, I pull open the nightstand drawer for a condom. She grabs it out of my hand, and tears the wrapper open with her teeth. She rolls it over my cock, and I don't remember the last time a woman has done that.

I lean down and she sits up at the same time. What the hell is she doing. A push to my shoulder as she maneuvers out from under me, and I know she wants me on my back. Whatever the lady wants, she gets.

As soon as I'm lying down, she straddles me, and leans down until her lips catch mine. I can't stop the moan I release. Fuck, this woman will be my undoing.

Moving one hand between us, she pulls away and grips my cock until she's sliding onto me. I guess the shyness from earlier is gone. She's out to take what she wants, and I can only be happy it's from me.

She rocks into me, torturing me as she takes her time. Fingernails grip into my shoulders, and I don't know how long I'm going to last. Leaning down she kisses my neck, jawline, and works her way to my ear. Her teeth catch my lobe, and my hands move to ass, quickening the pace. My ears are my weakness, and it didn't take her long to find it.

With one hand, she reaches down and rubs her clit between us. All it does is bring me closer to the edge. "Joan, I don't know how much longer I can last."

"I'm almost there." She pants against my ear before muffling her moans into my shoulder. Her teeth are scraping against my skin, and I can't hold back any longer. With her pulsing around me, I come wondering if it's too late to cancel all our plans for the day.

* * *

The fair is in full swing. People are milling about at various booths, checking out the handcrafted items. It's probably one of my favorite things about this event. Most of the vendors handmade the things they're selling, and they try to keep it that way to support our local artists.

I watch Joan take it all in. Her eyes are bouncing to each booth, trying to decide which she wants to visit first. The options can be overwhelming, especially for a newcomer. I know the first time Delilah dragged me here, I wasn't sure what to expect. But I'll be honest...I come for the food.

"Want to get a bite to eat before we see what all Asheville has to offer?"

"As long as we aren't doing any rides for a while." She looks down the row of food trailers and smokers. "I don't want to ruin the day by losing my lunch."

"It'll be a while before we make it to the rides."

"Then let's go." She moves through the crowd, checking out each food vendor.

"What are you in the mood for?"

She grips my hand and stops in her tracks as soon as she sees what she's looking for. "I didn't think places outside of the state fair had turkey legs and roasted corn."

"I take it that's what you want."

"Absolutely." She pulls me behind her as she makes her way toward the end of the lane where two huge smokers have a line of people in front of them. "It's the only reason I actually go to the fair, and I'm always sad it only lasts a month."

"I haven't been there since I was in high school, and we got free tickets and a day off from school."

"The kids have been bugging me about going this year already, and they don't start school for another month."

"Can you blame them?" The line is moving pretty quickly, but I keep all of my attention on Joan. I plan on making this relationship between us work, and her kids are part of the equation. I want to know about them. "It's the perfect day. No school, and fun."

"Yeah, I usually have to save up to go, but with the tips I've been getting, it won't be a problem this year. And it won't dip into Isaac's car fund."

"Wow."

"What?"

Shaking my head, I stand in awe of her. "Nothing. I didn't realize you had a soon-to-be driver. I'll be happy when my little brother can drive. Then I won't have to run him all over the place for his practices."

"Such is the life of a parent, or sibling. Isaac will need to help me out with Abby's practice schedules, but he says he doesn't mind. Now if I could actually get him to practice driving."

"I'm guessing he has no interest?"

"Nope. I'm not sure if he's scared of other people on the road, or he just doesn't want to do it." She throws her arms up in exasperation, "I don't know what is wrong with kids these days. Most of his friends don't want to drive either. When I was his age, I couldn't wait to learn. It offered a bit of freedom."

"My brother doesn't want to drive either. It definitely has to be a generational thing. I loved when I got my license, even if it was the beginning of being a chauffeur for my brother. My mom has always worked long hours, and I picked up the slack where I could."

"No wonder women find you irresistible."

The line moves and we take a few steps forward. "What's that supposed to mean?"

"You're the full package, even at a young age." She lets go of my hand and ticks off her fingers. "You have a steady job. Obviously, family is a big deal to you. And...you're sweet. Plus, protective. Honestly, I don't know how someone hasn't taken you off the market, yet."

"Maybe I'm the one who's been holding out. I knew there had to be someone who better suited me out in the universe." I grab hold of her hand again, ensuring she knows it's her I'm talking about.

She may have her doubts, but I don't have any. It's also probably too soon to even be thinking that way, but sometimes you just know. It's a gut feeling that won't go away. I had it the first time I saw her, and it only grew the more I got to know her.

It's our turn to place our order, and I wish there were more people in front of us. I need to hear what she has to say about what I just admitted.

"Do you want to share, or do we need to each get our own?" It doesn't matter either way to me. I'll do whatever makes her happy.

"I always tell my kids it's better to share. But...I typically only get this food once a year, and I'm not great about sharing my food."

"Fine by me." I tell the man behind the smoker we'll take two turkey legs and roasted corn.

He hands a foil wrapped leg to each of us before giving us the corn. He points to the side where the seasoning is placed for the corn. This moment is important. I need to see what seasonings she puts on her corn. She uses the spray butter first. Okay, we're on the same page. Then she studies the other items before picking up cajun seasoning and sprinkling it heavily on her corn. It's like we're two peas in a pod.

She follows me to tables that are lined up in the middle of the street under a set of canopies. Both of us sit at the same time and take a bite into the corn. She moans in appreciation. "You keep making those noises and we'll go right back to my house."

"I can't help it. This is my favorite fair food, and I get to have it before October."

"Fair point."

We eat in silence for a few moments and I want to ask her when I'll get to meet her kids. I know we're still in the early stages of dating, and despite what my mom advised, it'll make us feel official. Who's to say she won't drop me for a guy closer in age to her?

Joan is oblivious to the struggle I'm having, and looks around for a place to set her finished corn on the cob. "I wish I would have thought to bring a bag. There's no way I'm going to finish this turkey leg before we move on to the next thing."

"Give me a few minutes." I stand and look around to the closest booth. Most of the vendors have a bag of some sort. I rush over to a person selling notebooks and ask for a bag. She graciously gives me one, and I make my way back to the table. "Ask and you shall receive."

"Thanks." Her smile is wide as she takes the bag and puts it on her lap. "My eyes were definitely bigger than my stomach."

I watch her as she takes a few bites of her turkey leg. I do the same, and realize I won't be able to finish mine either. "Looks like I'm having the same problem."

She wraps up her food, opens the bag and places it inside. "Snack for later?"

"Absolutely." I add mine to the bag and take it from her. Today is about her and I won't make her carry this around all day. "Where do you want to go next?"

"Why don't we start there?" She points to the booth I

got the bag from. "It looks like they may have some stuff my daughter would like."

I follow her to the booth and hang to the side while she looks at the notebooks on display. They pages are sewn in by hand, and the covers are leather with varying designs. She finds a small one she likes, and pays for it before I get a chance to pull out my wallet.

The next few booths don't have anything to hold our interest and we make our way down the line. The day is warming up, and we'll need to take breaks before long. Otherwise we'll end up sunburnt and dehydrated.

We stop at a vendor who sells candles. They are brave selling these in the summer. It's going to be a scorcher, and I can't help but wonder if the wax will melt. I find a large one with flowers poking out of the wax, and know my mom would love it. As I pay, I feel Joan grab onto my shirt before ducking behind me.

"What's wrong?"

"My kids are here. Shit."

Maybe this is my chance to meet them. It's not like I'm going out of my way. Fate has placed them here at the same time we are. That has to mean something.

18

joan

OF ALL THE places Keith could take the kids this weekend, he decides to bring them here. Why didn't Abby text me with a warning. She knows I planned on being in this area today.

"Why are you hiding? We can go say hi." Eric doesn't seem to understand how badly that will go.

Even though Keith and I have a great co-parenting relationship, I haven't mentioned seriously dating anyone to him. The only one who knows is Abby. She doesn't need to be put in the middle of whatever fallout could potentially happen.

"My ex-husband, nor my son, know anything about you. I can't guarantee it would be a happy introduction."

This is the problem with dating someone far younger than me. He doesn't understand the nuances of dating with children. The wrench it can throw in their lives, and the distrust they could have toward me. I know I probably should have mentioned it to Isaac. I've never been one to hide things from them. But...this feels like a time to wait until things pan out how they are going to happen.

"I don't think you're giving them enough credit. They have to know you won't be single forever."

"My daughter knows. Well, she guessed and asked me about it before the game yesterday."

"Okay." He moves away from the booth. "We can head back to the car if you want."

"Yes." I nod and turn back in the direction of the car. "That sounds like a good idea."

"Mom." The decision is ripped out of my hands. Isaac's voice floats above the rest of the crowd and I know this isn't going to go well. Should I try to rush us along and pretend I didn't hear him? No. I can't do that. He'd never forgive me.

"Damn it." Turning around to the sound of my name, I wait for my former husband and kids to approach me. Eric stands beside me, but slightly behind. He is out of his element when it comes to this, and I feel horrible for putting him in the position.

Abby's eyes are wide, and she mouths a quick sorry in my direction. It's not her place to have to say sorry. I should have told Isaac and their dad I was dating. He's never let it be a secret when he's dating, and I feel like I've betrayed the trust we've built through the years of coparenting.

"Fancy seeing you here," Keith grins as he approaches us. "I didn't know you'd be out here today." Hmph. I bet he didn't. He knows this is the town I work in.

"Not as surprised to see you." It's an unnecessary dig, but I'm on edge.

Keith shrugs his shoulders. "I figured we'd get out of the city for a bit, and I saw something about this fair online. I was hoping to try out the bar and grill you work at, but was bummed to see they aren't open on Sundays."

"We like to give our employees a break, and we don't have to be open on Sunday." Eric adds in his two cents. I don't blame him. He's one of the managers and takes a lot of pride in the bar.

"Oh, do you own the bar?" Keith asks. His eyes bounce between the two of us trying to puzzle out why we're here together.

"No," Eric shakes his head. "I'm a manager, but Angie & Carlos take care of us."

"I see." He says as his eyes widen, and he figures it out. It's not that hard considering our proximity. He turns toward the kids and hands them some money. "Why don't y'all grab a snack." After they run off in the direction of the food trucks. His attention falls on me. "Joan, can we talk for a moment?"

Eric takes a step forward, but with a shake of my head he stands down. He doesn't know the dynamics of our family unit. How could he? I've shut down any sort of conversation he's wanted to have about the kids. Maybe I should have filled him in.

I follow Keith to an open space, and wait until he turns around to face me. "What do you have to say, Keith?"

"You realize he's practically a child, right?" I knew this was coming. It shouldn't since I haven't said anything about some of the women he's dated, or brought around the kids. It's his heart, and how he chooses to go about it is on him.

"Not that it's really any of your business, but he's in his mid-twenties. I don't understand why it matters."

"I'm just making sure you know what you're getting yourself into. Most kids his age know nothing about dating single parents." The way he puts emphasis on kid is annoying, and the fact he refers to Eric that way.

"Look, I don't judge your dating decisions, and I'd like the same in return. You don't know anything about him."

"Do Isaac and Abby know anything about him, yet?"

"No." It's not entirely true. "Well, Abby guessed I was seeing someone. She noticed a change in my mood, and put two and two together. Isaac doesn't know."

"You should probably tell him soon. You know he doesn't like being taken off guard." He's not wrong. He didn't handle our divorce well, and even though he's cordial to whomever Keith is dating...he doesn't exactly like them.

"I was waiting to make sure something was going to turn out from this before I said anything, but I'll talk to him tomorrow night when they come home."

"Okay," he runs a hand through his hair. "Sorry I over-reacted, it just took me by surprise."

"I get it," a soft laugh escapes. "He took me by surprise too."

"Abby is right, though. You look happier, and less stressed."

"Thanks." I think. "We can head out if you want to enjoy the day with the kids."

"It's okay," he waves my comment away. "I was going to let them ride a few rides before we headed out. They want to go bowling with their friends."

"Be prepared to separate them because the competitiveness is absurd."

"You're not telling me anything I don't know." He gestures to the spot we just left. "Shall we?"

We turn back to the area we left Eric, and I'm shocked to find him talking to the kids. Hopefully he hasn't told them anything I'm not ready for them to know.

"Hey, what did you get?" Keith asks as we approach them.

Abby holds out a plate. "Funnel cake. I think it might be better than anything I've ever tasted."

She tears off a piece and holds it out to her dad. He takes it and nods. "You know, you might be right." He holds out a hand to Eric. "I'm Keith, it's nice to meet you."

Eric warily takes Keith's hand and shakes. "Eric, likewise."

They release hands at the same time, and Keith points down the street. "Want to see what rides they have?"

"Yes," the reply at the same time, "bye, Mom." They give me a quick hug and take off down the road, powdered sugar floating in the air behind them.

"Y'all are more than welcome to join us for bowling later." Keith watches Eric to see how he'll react.

"I'll leave that up to Joan."

"Sounds good," he gives a quick wave. "I'll have the kids home when you get off work tomorrow."

"Thanks." I let out a sigh of relief once he's a few yards away from us, following our kids to the area with the rides. "So that was fun."

"Agreed," he laughs and shakes his head. "I mean, I wanted to meet them, but not quite under these circumstances."

"So, what were y'all talking about?" I need to make sure he didn't say anything about being my boyfriend, or whatever we are.

"Nothing really." He shrugs his shoulders and takes my hand now that they are out of view. "They told me about what sports they played, and asked who I was." He glances over at me and smirks. "Don't worry, I told them we were friends. Though, I think your daughter knows something."

"She does. She guessed yesterday." Hopefully her brother wasn't paying attention to her facial expressions.

"I also told them I have a brother their age, and maybe they could get together."

Huh. That's a nice way to ease him being around the kids. Why didn't I think of that? The fact they talked to him and were cool gives me a bit of hope. But I won't run away with that until after I talk to Isaac. He's the one who could throw a wrench in everything, and I'll always choose my kids above anything else. I only hope Eric understands that.

"We'll see." I squeeze his hand, relishing in the fact he didn't back off when Keith gave him side-eye. I know my ex-husband ended up not saying anything else on the matter today, and I hope it stays that way. This doesn't need to become a battle.

"Want to do more shopping?"

A little retail therapy will help calm the nerves. "Absolutely."

* * *

We waited as long as possible to come to the rides and games area to avoid running into my kids again. Not because I don't want to see them, but because I don't want them to see me and Eric being affectionate.

"Look, there's the rest of the Ashes crew." He points toward a crowd huddled in front of a basketball game. "Let's see what they're up to."

We walk hand in hand toward our co-workers. Carlos and Angie are arguing with each other. Patrick is shaking his head in the background, and our fellow bartenders are staring at the scene before them.

"What's going on?" I ask Lisa as we join the group.

"Angie and Carlos both think they are better than the

other at shooting hoops." She rolls her eyes and continues watching. "Honestly, I've never seen either of them do anything athletic. Well, maybe Carlos when we tosses the football with Caroline's son."

The son in question is doing his best not to laugh. I'm guessing he doesn't think Carlos is very good either.

Eric holds the bags out to me, "hold these for a second?"

"Sure." I take the bags and watch him approach our bosses.

"Let's make this interesting." He points to himself then Angie and Carlos, "whoever scores the least in points, supplies breakfast for the staff...winner's choice."

Lisa leans closer to me, "It's like he wants to see who he can piss off more."

"Do you think he'll win?" I've never seen Eric play a sport either, but I know for a fact he runs after this morning.

"For sure." She laughs.

We watch the three of them line up in front of the goals. There's a set separating each one. Patrick goes behind Eric to count. Caroline is behind Carlos, and Dylan with Angie. Maybe they shouldn't have their partners count for them, but I'm not throwing in my two cents. I'm the new kid on the block.

The person running the booth blows a whistle and the three of them grab a ball and shoot. It would have been more entertaining if they were all shooting into the same goal, but this is probably the best way to keep it fair.

Eric isn't even paying attention to what his bosses are doing. His eyes completely focused on the goal. It reminds me of this morning when his gaze never left mine as I fell apart. Okay, Joan, calm down those thoughts. You're in public.

I'm not sure how much time has passed, maybe a minute, but the whistle blows and all three have set down the ball in their hands. The person running the booth has Patrick, Dylan and Caroline approach him. They give them their totals and return their spots. The vendor walks to Eric, grabs his arms and lifts it in the air. "We have a winner."

All of us cheer for him, and he hams it up. He's definitely not a graceful winner. The vendor then goes to Carlos, and says, "Sorry, but looks like you're buying breakfast."

"No way," he groans. "There's no way Angie beat me."

"What can I say?" She blows on her knuckles and scrubs them across her shoulder. "I'm a badass."

"Whatever," Carlos rolls his eyes, and turns to Eric, "let me know what you decide and I'll have it there tomorrow morning."

"Can't wait," Eric grins. He follows the vendor to the side of the basketball goals and digs around for something. The rest of the group says they're goodbyes and part ways. Each of the couples heading in different directions.

I watch them for a few moments before looking to the sky. The sun is setting and we're losing time. We can't stay out all night since I have to get up earlier than normal to make it to my weekday job on time.

A few moments later Eric approaches me with his hands behind his back. What in the world?

"Here you go." He pulls his hands in front of him, and waits for my reaction. Uncertainty flashes across his face.

In his hand is a small stuffed bear holding a basketball. I guess being the winner of the game also meant he got to pick out a prize. I set the bags on the ground, careful to keep them from spilling. "Thank you." I grab it out of his hands. "I love it."

And I do. Never have I had someone give me something they won. Even if he did it to beat his bosses, I'll cherish it for the sweet gift it is.

19

eric

AS SOON AS I present the bear to Joan, I feel like an idiot. This isn't something grown men do. At least, I don't think they do. The new territory I'm wading into is terrifying, but worth it.

But seeing her happy with the prize, is enough to ease some of my anxiety over it. "The rides are still open for a little while longer, want to see what they have?"

"Sure." She hugs the bear to her chest, and I pick up the bags from the ground. "Nothing that spins, though. I'm not a huge fan of those."

"Got it." I take a few steps and she works herself under my arm. "Would the ferris wheel be okay?"

"That's actually perfect." She looks down at the bags in my hands. "Where are we going to put our stuff?"

"I'm sure there's someone I know that would be willing to keep an eye on it. Or I can see if the attendant will let me stash it behind the controls."

"Wow. People really just do whatever you want?"

"What can I say?" I shrug my shoulders and pull her further into me. "I've got charm."

"Wow, you think pretty highly of yourself."

"It's how I get through life. You should try it."

I lead her over to the ferris wheel. The line is long. I'm pretty sure it's because most people waited until the sun was down so they could get a ride while the lights were on. The view of our tiny town is a romantic backdrop for the evening. It's one of the reasons I waited so long for us to do the rides. It's the moment I've been waiting for.

We watch the people getting on and off the ride. Most are couples on a date. The ages vary from high school all the way up to those who have no doubt spent decades together.

Finally, we reach the front of the line. I bought tickets earlier, and hand them over to the person running the ride. "Can I set these back here until we're back?"

The attendant nods, and I set them down. He points us to the open cart where another person waits to make sure we are fastened in. Holding my hand out to Joan, I help her into the seat before sitting beside her. We lift our hands to our chest so the attendant can close the latch. He gives it a tug to make sure it's not going to open, and signals a thumbs up before moving out of the way.

Within a minute we're moving forward. The sudden jolt is a bit frightening, but I know we're okay. Her hand squeezes mine and she leans her head against my shoulder. "Thank you for today. I've had a lot of fun."

"Really?" I could tell she did, but confirmation helps. "I didn't know if the whole small town fair thing was your vibe since you're from the city and used to grand events."

"No, this is exactly my speed. It's also nice seeing people we've served at the bar. It's like a slice into their life when they aren't dancing and hanging out."

"Definitely a perk of living in a small town. The one I grew up in is about twenty minutes away. It's slightly bigger than Asheville, but still has the same feeling."

"You don't see yourself living in the city at all?"

Is she wondering if things progress with us, or is this just a question to pass the time? "I don't know. I've never really lived in one. I go from time to time to hang out with old school friends, but as far as living there...I couldn't say."

"Understandable. It can be a lot." She sighs and cuddles closer to me despite the warm night. "I can see myself living in a place like this. The slower pace, and tight community, are things I've always wanted for my kids."

That's good to know. There's a possibility of us being closer together. "You can always look for places here in Asheville. They have houses for sale a few streets over from mine."

She laughs, "it's a little too soon for me to start looking for houses near yours. Besides, my kids have school coming up, and Isaac doesn't handle change well."

"You never know," I place my other hand on her knee, "this could be a change he needs."

"Or it could be disastrous. I'm honestly surprised he talked to you when we ran into them earlier. He has to know on some level that we're more than friends."

"It's possible," I lean over and kiss the top of her head. "But you will eventually need to tell him you're dating."

"I plan on it."

"Good. He may take it better than you expect."

I can feel her roll her eyes. She's right, though. I talked to the kid for less than five minutes, and I don't know him the same way she does.

"I plan on talking to him tomorrow evening. Probably

after baseball practice because I don't want to do anything that could make that go badly."

"Probably smart." Rushing it on my end isn't going to do anything. I need to let her do it at her own pace. Hopefully she really does talk to him, though.

Shifting my weight, I pull my phone out of my pocket. "What are you doing?" Joan squeals as the seat moves.

"Capturing our first real date." I hold the camera in front of us, hoping like hell I don't drop it. "We'll want to remember this when we're old and gray, and telling our grandkids of how we hit it off."

"You're very presumptuous." I take a photo of her staring up at me.

I bend down and press my lips to hers. Another photo. "I like to think of it as optimistic."

It's the only way I get through life. If I think of all the hard things and let that hold me back, I won't be able to do great things. Some may look down at me for my job, but I make people smile while I'm behind that bar. They know they can come to me with whatever is bothering them, and I'll give them a listening ear.

The ferris wheel moves around slowly, and we remain silent the rest of the ride. Taking in the sounds of music playing around us, and the crowd below chattering excitedly. Other than unexpectedly running into her kids and ex-husband, today is the best day I've ever spent with a woman. I only hope it leads to more like it.

* * *

"Why are you up so early?" Joan grumbles in my ear. "My alarm hasn't gone off yet."

"I know." I lean on my arm beside her. These past two

nights are the best sleep I've gotten in ages. Well, when we actually fell asleep late into the night. "I was trying to be nice."

"By waking me up before I have to be functional?" She turns on her side and moves until her back is flush against my chest. "I need my beauty sleep."

"You're already beautiful."

"It's too early for you to be cheesy." She grabs one of the pillows and pulls it over her head.

"Fine, I'll let you sleep." Her alarm will go off in about forty-five minutes, and I want to make sure she has a good start to the day. Her breathing has evened out, and I know she won't wake up.

Sliding out of the bed, I do my best not to jostle the sheets. In the dark, I make my way to the dresser and pull out a shirt. I have no idea what color is, and I don't care. I'm just happy I have my room memorized, otherwise I would have made noise and woken her up again.

I crack the door open enough for me to slip through before softly closing it behind me. Our bags from yesterday are on the kitchen table, and I sort through them. I have a couple of reusable bags in the pantry and I grab one to put her things into. There's no sense in her carrying a bunch of bags when she can take one.

The house is silent and I wish I could put on some music, but I don't want to wake her. I'm not sure how heavy of a sleeper she is, but I don't want to chance it. Moving my stuff to the coffee table, I finish cleaning off the one in the kitchen.

It's a good thing I bought groceries before she came to stay for the weekend. I plan on sending her off with a good breakfast and coffee. I set two plates on the table and a fork. I can't make a lot of things, but I'm pretty good at eggs since it's what I eat pretty much every morning after my run. Which I'll have to do after she leaves. I don't want to miss a moment with her, and I know we won't be able to do this again for another two weeks.

As quietly as possible, I pull out the pans I'll need to cook. A baking sheet slips and I catch it before it clatters to the ground. Damn, I'm not used to needing to be quiet in my own house. I place it on the counter and turn to the fridge to get everything else.

Eggs, bell pepper, jalapenos, milk, and biscuits now cover the counter beside the stove. The only thing I need now is a bowl. Pulling it down I crack a few eggs inside and mix it with a dash of milk. In a small skillet I mix together the bell pepper and jalapeños, sautéing them until they are soft.

I set them aside until I need them. Pulling open the drawer by the coffee pot, I grab two pods and set them next to the pot. I don't want to start it just yet. Cold coffee is not my jam. I place the biscuits on the cookie sheet and slide them into the oven.

With all of that done, I prepare the larger skillet for omelets, and start cooking. Lost in making breakfast, I startle when arms wrap around my waist. "It smells delicious."

"I hope I didn't wake you." Quiet isn't my strong suit, especially when I'm not used to having people here so early in the morning. It didn't affect much when Lisa lived here. That woman could sleep with a freight train blowing its horn in her ear.

"Nope. I woke up before my alarm. It's normal."

"That's good. I was trying to be as quiet as possible."

"You were." She lets go of me, and moves toward the coffee pot. "Is this for this morning?"

"Yeah, I was waiting until you got up to start it."

She opens the top and sets a pod inside, starting the brew. "I've got it. But please tell me you have creamer."

"In the fridge." I point toward it with the spatula. "I wasn't sure what you liked so I have regular, and a couple of flavored ones."

"You really do think of everything." She grins and gets the creamer.

"I wanted this weekend to be perfect."

"Oh, it has been." She hops up to sit on the counter by the sink. "I'm kind of bummed to go back to my other job today. I enjoy my job, but it doesn't give me the same rush working at the bar does."

"What do you mean?"

"I'm able to help people with problems they have with their accounts, but I don't get to know them on a personal level like I do here. It's different when you're seeing someone face to face."

She's right. It's one of the reasons I don't think I could ever work an office job. I like interacting with my customers. Knowing they are happy, or have someone to lean on when they need it.

"You could always come work here full time."

She's shaking her head when I glance over my shoulder. "No, I can't. I need to be able to be there for the kids' sports. And I can't do that if I 'm working nights."

"Angie and Carlos have always been very flexible. Especially now that Carlos has a family of his own."

"Yeah, but if they make concessions for me, they have to do it for everyone."

"They already do. Angie has always tried to keep things family oriented. It's why we're open during the day so people can enjoy lunch or an early dinner with their families." I move the last omelet to another dish. "They even let me take off when I need to for my brother."

"I'll think about it." I'm not sure if she's saying that to keep me from talking about it, or if it's because she really will think about it. I'm of the firm belief that if something brings you joy, especially in occupation, you should do it. "Let's eat so I can get ready for work. The drive is a lot longer from here."

She hops off the counter and grabs the plates from the table to load them up with food. I pull the biscuits out of the oven and pull down another coffee cup to make mine. I watch as she adds french vanilla creamer to her coffee and adds sugar. Apparently, the creamer doesn't add enough sweetness. To each their own.

We don't talk much while we eat. Both of us in our thoughts, or mentally checking off the tasks we need to accomplish for the day. Once we're finished, she jumps in the shower, and I clean up the kitchen.

I'm in the room changing into my running clothes when she comes in wrapped in a towel. A replay of yesterday morning runs through my mind, but in reverse. "How am I supposed to focus for the rest of the day if you come in here with nothing on?"

"Think about it until the next time we see each other?" She smirks and grabs her clothes off the bed. "I can't take much longer, I'll hit traffic as it is."

"Grab what you need from the bag, and I'll load up your car while you finish getting ready."

"Thanks," she breathes a sigh of relief. Throwing everything aside from what she's wearing today into the bag she hands it over.

"I'll be right back." With the bag in hand, I rush to the

kitchen and start another cup of coffee. I'll switch it over to a travel mug she can take with her.

Grabbing her keys off the counter, I get her other bag full of items she bought yesterday and head to her car. It doesn't take long to load it. She travels light. Once I'm back inside, I transfer the coffee into a travel mug, and add her creamer and sugar.

She emerges from the bedroom, purse in hand. "I guess it's time for me to go."

"I'll walk you out." With her coffee in hand, I open the front door and wait for her to go ahead of me.

She turns when she gets to her car door and throws her arms around my neck. "Thank you for an amazing weekend."

"Anytime." I give her a quick kiss before backing up. "You are going to be late."

"Probably." She opens the door and slides into the driver's seat.

"Here, I made this for the road."

She looks up at me, eyes wide, and smiles. "A girl could get used to this."

"Play your cards right and it could be an everyday thing." I close the car door and watch her back out of the driveway. She's my forever, even if she doesn't realize it yet.

20

joan

IT'S BEEN a week since my weekend with Eric. This may be the most I've ever texted and called someone in my life. While I'm good with technology, I much prefer face to face interactions. Things don't get lost in translation that way.

"Have you talked to Isaac, yet?" Keith is sitting beside me in the bleachers while we watch our son play.

My dad, on the other side of me, interjects the conversation. "No, she hasn't."

"I thought you were going to do it Monday night?" Keith stares at me in confusion. "The longer you put it off, the more likely it's not going to go well. Especially if he thinks you've been lying to him."

"I know." I wish the two of them would stop. "It's hard because what if things don't work out between us and then it's a heartbreak for them as well as me?"

Dad pats my shoulder. "That's part of life, Bug. You can't shelter yourself or them. All you can do is be there for them if things don't go as planned."

If anyone is an expert in this, it's him. He handled things like a pro when Mom split. I barely even remember her now. This is different, though. It's not someone leaving the family, never to be seen again. This is me potentially adding someone to our group. And if I have it my way, it'll be forever. What if they can't come to terms with that?

"Will it make you feel better if I'm there when you talk to them?" Keith asks.

"Maybe?" Honestly, at this point it's probably the only way it's going to happen.

"She's off work tomorrow." Dad points out. "Y'all can tell him at lunch so you have the rest of the day to talk it over if you need to."

"Fine." I pout even though I know I'm being ridiculous. "Tomorrow at lunch. I'll order pizza or something to make it less traumatizing for the kids."

"I'll bring the pizza," Keith says. "You just figure out what you're going to say."

"Okay." There's no point arguing. Both of them have given reasonable responses, and even though neither of them are excited about the age difference, they trust my judgment.

I can only hope Isaac takes it well. If he doesn't, I'm not sure what I'm going to do. Eric makes me happy. I mean, I was happy before, but he adds to the small joys in life. Things I didn't realize I missed so much. He gets excited when I tell him how Isaac is doing in baseball. He's the optimistic side to my realistic personality. It's not because he's never seen hardship. He's shared some of his childhood. He may get it more than anyone I've dated.

"Do the kids have anyone staying over tonight?" Dad bumps into my shoulder.

"Not that I know of, but I wouldn't rule it out." Both

Isaac and Abby are horrible about having people come over at the last minute.

"I'll stop by the grocery store and get some snacks just in case." All of our eyes are on Isaac as he walks to the plate to bat. "But I'll be sure to tell them nobody can stay the night. Their friends need to be picked up tonight."

"Sounds good. Or you can just tell them no when they ask."

"Grandparent's perk is I don't have to tell them no." He points to me and Keith, "that's your job."

Good ol' Dad. Doing anything and everything to keep from being the bad guy. Isaac swings and misses. The pitcher throws the ball and he gets a hit off it. It's not enough to get him past second base, but one of his team-mates is able to run in. We all stand and cheer.

As happy as I am watching my son play, I know without a doubt I'll be playing over what will happen tomorrow for the rest of the day.

* * *

"Is everything okay?" Eric asks as he grabs a bottle of tequila from the shelf behind me.

"Yeah, just a lot on my mind." I'm pouring a beer for the customer in front of me. It's early, and we haven't gotten busy yet. Families are grabbing dinner before they head home for the night.

"Anything I can help with?"

"Not really."

Eric doesn't know that I haven't talked to Isaac yet. Anytime he's brought up the subject, I've steered it in another direction. I should tell him, I know that. But I'm worried it will cause some grief between us. Right now, that's not something I'm willing to risk.

"Okay, well let me know if you change your mind." He gives me that grin that makes all my defenses crumble. "I'm pretty good at listening."

He's not wrong. Anytime I've needed to vent about work, or the kids fighting, he's been right there, lending me an ear. I hope I've been able to do the same when he comes to me. It's usually about his brother. It's not like I can offer a lot of advice since I'm usually in the same boat with my kids.

"I will." Let's be honest, I'll end up talking to him about it before the end of the night. He really is the one person I want to turn to. Lisa will listen, but she doesn't really get it. There's always Carlos, but he was the one added in. Actually, I may talk to him. He will know how to handle this. What I should say, and all that jazz. It'll be nice to have an outside perspective.

The rest of the afternoon goes by quickly. We've had a steady stream of customers, but nothing too outlandish. I know that will change as the sun goes down and people are ready to decompress.

My eyes search the bar for Carlos, I know it's almost time for him to get off work. They have little league football tonight. So, Eric was right. They do make family a priority. I saw Angie's name on the board, so I assume she's coming in to cover him for a couple of hours.

Finally, I see him heading down the hall to the office. Now's my chance. If I don't go now, I won't be able to get his insight before my talk with Isaac. I get Lisa's attention. "I'm going to take my break. You good?"

"Yep. Go get some downtime before the rush starts." She shifts until she's in the middle of our sections.

Normally she handles the drinks that come from those ordering food, but she's always good to fill in for me when needed.

I make my way around the bar and head down the hallway. The door is ajar, but I still knock so I know I'm not intruding on a conversation. I've heard the stories of folks just walking in, only to find some of my coworkers making out. That's not something I want to see.

"Come in," Carlos calls. From the sound of his voice, he's at the computer.

I push the door open and step inside. I don't close the door all the way because I don't think it will take long. "Can I talk to you for a minute?"

"What did Eric do?" He's already shaking his head, wondering if he's going to lose an employee.

"Nothing. Eric and I are good." Pulling out the chair in front of the desk, I take a seat. "I was actually looking for advice."

"I'm not good at dating advice." He holds his hands up.

"No, it's not that." I laugh and push aside his concern. "How did you handle things when you met Caroline's son? More specifically, was there anything you or she did to prepare him to meet you?"

"I take it you haven't told your kids yet."

"Nope. Well, my daughter guessed I was seeing someone. But I haven't told my son. We did run into them at the fair last weekend when they were with their dad, but he hasn't mentioned anything about it."

He leans back in his chair and crosses his arms over his chest. "Your kids are older, right?"

"Yeah, fourteen and almost sixteen."

"This may not help then." He takes a few moments to choose his words. "I'm not sure what conversations Caroline had with David before he met me. But when we did meet, it was at my mom's house. My sisters are about the same age as your kids, and provided a buffer if we needed it."

"How did that go?"

"Surprisingly well. My sisters adored him and he loved them. He even opened up to me while I was losing to him at horseshoes."

"So, I should orchestrate a playdate?"

"I don't know." He shrugs his shoulders and leans forward. "Your kids are older than David. But I think them meeting on level ground is probably a good idea. Invite Eric to a game, or something like that."

"Wait, is your ex-husband a total asshole?"

I'm guessing Caroline's is and that's the reason for the question. "Not at all. We co-parent the kids and are way better off this way."

"Okay, then as long as all parties are on board, you shouldn't have any issues."

Standing, I glance at my watch. I still have a few minutes for my break and I want to check in on the kids. "Thanks for answering my questions. I'm at a total loss most days."

"I think that's a lot of parents. I'm definitely learning a lot each day."

"Parenthood is a rollercoaster, that's for sure." I move toward the door. "But thank you. It means a lot."

I open the door only to find Eric outside. "You haven't told your son, yet?"

Shit. This wasn't how I wanted him to find out. I was actually hoping he wouldn't since it's happening tomorrow.

"No, I'm doing it tomorrow and wanted to get some

insight." Please let him understand my predicament.

"But you said you were going to talk to him about it earlier this week." I don't miss the hurt that crosses his face, and hate even more I'm the one who put it there. "Is it because you don't think things will work out?"

"Not at all." I glance past him to see if anyone is heading this direction. It's not exactly a conversation I want to have in front of a ton of people. "I was working out how to do it."

"It's not that hard, Joan. You talk to him."

"It's not that simple." I throw my hands in the air. "I didn't receive a manual when my kids were born telling me how to approach situations, much less introducing a boyfriend to older children. This is uncharted territory, and I'm trying to find the best way to navigate it."

"I can be there when you talk to him." He runs a hand through his hair. "Maybe that will make it easier."

"That's probably not a good idea." His eyebrows furrow and I know I've hit a nerve. He wants to be involved, and I'm telling him he can't be. Not with this.

"Okay." He doesn't say another word and goes back in the direction of the bar. It's at this moment I realize how much the age difference can be a problem. He didn't stay to talk anything else out. Just walked away. Maybe he only needs time to digest what I told him, or he didn't want to say anything out of frustration.

That's the way I'm going to take it. All I know is the rest of the evening is going to be tense.

* * *

My feet drag as I make my way to the coffee pot. Eric walked me to my car last night, but didn't say much. I can't help but feel like he's pulling away. Both of us could have handled the conversation better last night.

"Coffee doesn't go very well with pizza." My dad eyes me from the kitchen table and points to the boxes in front of him.

"Where's Keith?" I spent the morning getting ready for next week and didn't even hear him come in.

"In the backyard with the kids." He sets his water down. "I don't' know how he's going to throw the ball to both of them considering they play completely different sports."

"I'm sure he's managing." I pour the leftover coffee from the pot into a cup. Not even bothering with sugar or creamer, I take a sip. Why do people drink it this way? It's not horrible, but it's also not good.

"You ready to do this?"

"Not really, but I might as well get it over with." After last night, it may not even matter. But I need to be honest with the kids. They deserve that much.

Dad gets up from the table to get the kids and I grab some plates from the cabinet. I take a deep breath with each one I get out. I kept waiting for Eric to text me some sort of positive text for today, but he never did. I guess I'm on my own.

Everyone comes in from the backyard and we all take our seats around the table. The kids are the first to dig into the pizza boxes, piling their plates high. I'll never understand how the two of them can eat so much.

Once everyone's plates are full, Keith glances over at me and nods. Taking one last deep breath, I do what I know I've needed to for the past few weeks. "Isaac, Abby. There's something I need to tell you."

Abby gives me an encouraging nod. I think she knew

what we had planned as soon as she found out we were having a day together. Isaac watches me, waiting to see what I have to say.

Before I lose my nerve, I blurt it all out. "I'm seeing someone. I have been for a few weeks, but you both need to know. There are times when you're at your dad's, I won't be home. I need to know you're okay with it."

"Why wouldn't we be?" I expected the question to come from Abby, but it's Isaac who asks the question.

"I don't know. I know our divorce wasn't easy on you and I didn't want to say anything until I knew something would come out of it."

"It's the guy we saw you with at the fair, right?" He asks and takes another bite.

"Yes."

"Cool. He's really nice." This isn't the reaction I thought I would get. Especially from Isaac.

"And you're okay with it?" Keith interjects. No doubt wanting to make sure he isn't just saying things to appease me.

"Yeah." He rolls his eyes and takes another bite. Once he's finished chewing, he adds, "I'm not a little kid anymore mom. I have friends on my team who have divorced parents. After we saw you, I figured that's what was happening."

"Why didn't you say anything?"

"I knew you'd say something when you wanted to."

"Well, okay." Eric was right. My kids will surprise me in ways I never know. Isaac can also handle more than what I thought he could. "Do you want to talk about it? Or meet him officially?"

"No offense, Mom, but I don't need to know about your dating life. Keep it to yourself like Dad does." He shakes his head. "I do want to meet him…just not today. Can I meet up with the guys to practice a bit?"

"Um sure."

"I'll take you wherever you need to go, kiddo." Keith ruffles Isaac's hair and our son grimaces. "Just let your mom know when she needs to pick you up."

That wasn't as difficult as I thought it would be. Maybe I'm not so bad at this whole teenage mom thing as I thought I was. I can't wait to tell Eric.

21

eric

WAS I dick to Joan at work last night? Yes. Do I regret it? Also, yes. I let my emotions get the best of me. She's telling her son about us today, and I should be happy about it. But I can't help the annoyance I feel. She never mentioned not telling him earlier in the week like she said she would.

'Why do you look mad at the world?" Mom asks me as we sit down for lunch. Cameron is looking at his phone as Mom gets everything sorted on the table.

"Just stuff with Joan." I'll be lucky if she doesn't hit me upside the head when she pulls the story out of me.

"What did you do?" She yanks the phone out of Cameron's hand and puts it face down on the table away from him. "You know the rule. No phones while we're eating."

"You could have asked," he argues. "You didn't have to grab it out of my hands."

"Do I pay for it?"

"Yes."

"Then I can do as I want. Be happy I'm not like those other parents who dig through their kids' phones."

She has a point. I've heard those horror stories from parents at the bar. Both from those that do this, and the others that don't. "At least you know you can go to her for anything, and she doesn't need to snoop because of that relationship."

"Why are you changing the subject, big bro? Sounds like you're buttering her up before you admit what you did."

"Shut up." I kick his leg under the table and he winces.

"Yes, Eric. What did you do?"

"Why does it have to be something I did?" Offended, I take a bite of the sandwich she's made.

My brother snickers and winces again. I guess mom kicked him that time. "Because you are impatient and want everything to happen on your timeline."

She's not wrong. I knew Angie and Carlos were looking for someone to promote, and I worked my ass off to get it. I may have all bugged them every other day. But it's always worked out for me in the past. Which is why it stings so badly that it hasn't worked the way I wanted it to this time.

Joan and I aren't broken up, but since I overheard her talking to Carlos last night, it feels like things aren't the same. Also, my fault. Why did I get so defensive?

"Tell me what happened?" Mom leans forward with her hands clasped, her food all but forgotten.

"Do I have to do it while he's here?" I point to my little brother. The need to look like I have my shit together for him is important to me. Something for him to aspire to.

"It's good for him to know that things in life are hard." Mom says. I guess there's no way of getting out of this. I relay what happened last weekend. From how amazing our weekend was to running into her family. Then finally to overhearing her conversation with Carlos, and my reaction afterward.

"Did you pressure her to talk to her kids when you were at the fair?" Of course, that's what she'd lead with.

"No, Mom. We were heading back to the car after she saw them to avoid it, but her son saw her first. I didn't say anything about us dating. I just told them I was a friend from work."

"That's good." She thinks for a moment, choosing her words before saying them aloud. "Why did you react so badly at work last night? You should be happy she's telling them."

That's a good question. I'm not sure why I did. Okay, yes, I do, but I don't want to admit it. "I don't know."

Mom gives me a look. "Yes, you do."

"Fine. I felt like her putting it off meant that what I feel toward her isn't the same way she feels toward me."

"Why didn't you tell her that?"

"For the same reason I didn't want to talk about this in front of Cameron." I point to the person in question. "I don't like people seeing that side of me."

"You're allowed to be vulnerable. And you should. Especially with those you love. They should be able to see all of you." She sits back in her chair, tapping her fingers in a steady rhythm. "Do you love her?"

I've never felt this way about any other person I've been with. I mean, I love Lisa, but as a sister. She's my best friend. I've avoided talking to her about Joan because they are also friends, and I didn't want to cause friction. But when I'm away from Joan, I can't get her off my mind. I text her throughout the day to check on her and the kids. To see if they need anything, or just to show her how much she means to me. I see her in my future no matter how I look at it. Even if we don't live in the same city for now, I know she's it for me. I've thought about looking at houses, or apartments, in her area just to be closer to her. Holy crap. I do love her.

"I think I fell a little in love with her before she took me seriously. And now it only grows with each day."

"Then you need to fix this."

She's right. I know she is, but I need some reassurance from her that we can be together. No more dancing around the issue of our futures, or what obstacles we're facing. We need to have a no-nonsense discussion.

"I plan on it."

"Good." She nods and finally eats her food. "Now hurry up and finish your lunch so you can go home and figure things out."

This is the problem with having a close relationship with your mom. It seems like she gets bossier the older you get.

* * *

The Monday morning staff meeting is long. Stella and Angie asked us to be here an hour earlier than normal, and I'm dragging. Last night I kept running different scenarios in my head, trying to pick the one that would be the most effective. I'm still at a loss.

Stella is going on and on about events she wants us to hold in the Fall. She mentions something about a Halloween party, and from the look on Patrick's face, he has no interest in that. "I know it's during the week, but I want all hands-on deck. Or we could possibly move it to the weekend before. Whatever works for everyone."

"You realize that's still like two months away, right?" I shouldn't have said anything because her glare turns my way.

"Yes, I do. But we need to plan and sell tickets. Which is why are planning for it now. Is there anyone that won't be able to make it?"

Patrick raises his hand like a kid in school. "I may or may not be here. I'm not sure if I'm going out of town yet."

Ooo, I wonder what he has going on. He's been acting weird lately, and that has to be the reason. I make a mental note to ask him about it later.

Stella and Angie make note of it on the pieces of paper in front of them. "Anyone else?"

When nobody answers, Stella talks about other events she wants us to have. I tune her out. Either way I'll be here for all of it. Once Stella's announcements are done, Angie begins her pep talk. It's like they are good cop, bad cop. Angie pumps us up, while Stella gives us the breakdown of how things are going to go.

Carlos walks in carrying bags in his hands. I wondered where he was. He never misses these meetings. He falls in line with Stella's approach to them. I already know if we have the Halloween party on the actual night, Carlos is out. They have trick-or-treating to do with David.

He sets the bags on the table. "Breakfast tacos per the winner's request."

Dang, I totally forgot I told him what I wanted for us. I figured he'd bring it the next day, but the meeting makes sense. It's the one time all of the employees are here, except for Joan since she has another job.

"Thanks." Everyone says in unison. We all dig in while Angie continues going over what's happening for the week, and what we need to do. Thank God the list isn't long.

Though she's always telling us if we find other people looking for work to send them her way. She wants to give us enough employees that we can take off whenever we need.

Now that the meeting is done, everyone forms their own little groups to talk and finish eating. Carlos pulls out a chair next to mine. "So how did the everything go with Joan's son yesterday?"

"I'm not sure." I kept waiting for her to let me know, but my phone never went off. I checked it the entire time I was at my mom's house. Not a single missed text or call.

"Oh." Carlos rubs his neck. "Hopefully it went well. Coming into a family isn't exactly the easiest."

"So, I've heard." If anyone knows it's him. He's gone through this with less than stellar circumstances. Caroline's ex-husband was kind of a jerk and didn't make things easy for either of them.

"Are things okay between the two of you?"

"Why do you ask?"

"You look like someone just kicked your puppy."

"Just a misunderstanding, but I plan on clearing it up as soon as I can." It sounds like it needs to be sooner rather than later. Also, I kind of hate that everyone can read me so easily. I guess it's because I'm always the happy one. The person who brings everyone else up.

"Good." Without another word he stands and walks over to Angie and Stella. He's looking at a paper Stella is holding and shaking his head. I'm guessing it's about Halloween and we'll be having the party on the weekend. Perks of being one of the bosses. He's part of the final call.

We have about an hour before we open, and I make my rounds to get everything cleaned up. Bands only play here on the weekend, so I go to the radio we have set up and pick a station to set the mood. Once indie alternative plays through the speakers, everyone else groans. They should have beat me to the radio.

Patrons trickle in as the day progresses. Our regulars are here for lunch and they order the same thing every time. It must be a comfort for them because I know I'd get tired of it. I help the waitstaff by refilling drinks and taking care of any tables they need me to.

An unexpected face shows up at the bar, and I pause wondering what the hell I did now. Joan's ex-husband is the last person I expected to see. He takes a seat in front of me, and leans his elbows on the table. "What can I get you?"

He doesn't even bother looking over the menu I slide in front of him. "Sweet tea and wings."

"Do you want fries with that?"

"Sure." Well, isn't he all warm and cuddly?

I put the order in with Patrick and get Keith his tea. A part of me wants to hang out in the kitchen for a bit. Whatever brought him here can't be good, and it most certainly has to do with Joan and their kids.

Before I chicken out, I bring Keith his tea and set it in front of him. "So, why do I have the pleasure of your company today?"

There's no need to beat around the bush. Better to get this confrontation out of the way so we can both get on with our day.

"What's going on with you and Joan? When we saw the two of you at the fair, she was happy and looked lighter than she has in a while. Then yesterday when we told our kids about her dating, she was upset."

We really need to be around people who can't read us so well. Now to figure out how to answer. "Well, I may have overreacted when I found out she hadn't told the kids about us yet. It leaned into an insecurity I had, and I didn't handle it well."

"Figures," he mutters just loud enough for me to hear. "Do you plan on figuring it out? Or, are you going to keep acting like a child about it?"

I see the dig for what it is. He doesn't think she should be dating someone my age. Too bad it's not his call. "I'm actually working on my plan right now."

"Good." Patrick interrupts us to set Keith's order in front of him. "I don't want to get involved in your relationship, but you need to know Joan is probably the best woman I've ever known, and she deserves the world." As much as I want to interject about him not being able to provide that for her, I don't. "She's happy with you, and you need to fix whatever is broken between you."

"Understood." He's giving a directive and not asking what I want to do. Making up with Joan is at the top of my list. I leave him to his lunch to serve another customer who sits on the other end of the bar. It doesn't take long, but when I come back with the bill his card is already out to pay.

I take it from him and process the payment before bringing it back to him for his signature. As I slide him the receipt, he hands me a napkin with writing. "If you really care about Joan, you'll make things right. That's where Isaac's tournament is this weekend."

"Um, thanks."

He signs his receipt and leaves. When I glance down at it, I'm shocked to see he left a decent sized tip. Maybe he doesn't hate me after all.

Since there's only one person at the bar now, and he's happily eating his lunch, I pull out my phone and send a text to Joan.

Eric: Will I see you at work this weekend?

Joan: Isaac has a tournament and it starts Friday night. I'm not on the schedule, but I'll be there sometime on Saturday.

Eric: See you then.

I know she's scheduled off for Friday, I'm the one who made it. But now...project apologize to Joan begins.

22

joan

OTHER THAN THAT bland text Eric sent me on Monday, I haven't heard from him most of the week. He gave me a heads up about a Halloween party the bar is throwing, but not much else. It sucks because I don't know where we stand. The radio silence is enough to drive me insane.

"Hey, Mom." Abby comes into the room. "Do I have to go to the tournament all weekend?"

We are supposed to leave in twenty minutes, and she asks me this now. I swear my kids have zero concept of time. "Why?"

"Chloe is having a sleepover and asked if I could come."

"And she planned it today?"

"Yep. She's asking a couple of other girls from the team to come so we can get some practice in before school starts. Camp wasn't exactly stellar with some of the players."

She knows I'm less likely to say no if they are doing it as

a team building sort of thing. And I have to admit I'm impressed the girls are putting this together instead of the coach. It shows some initiative.

"Fine. But her parents will have to pick you up. And, either me or your dad will be there in the morning to get you. This is your brother's last tournament before school starts and it would be nice if you're there."

"Thank you." She rushes to me and gives me a hug. "I'll be ready early. And don't worry everything will work out."

Ugh, the way this kid takes everything on is breaking my heart. She shouldn't be worrying about my heart as she goes into the school year.

"Don't you worry about me and Eric. We'll work things out one way or another." I squeeze her one last time because my baby is growing up faster than I want her to. "Go have fun with your friends. Fill me in on all the juicy gossip tomorrow."

"Oh, I will. You don't have to worry about that." She turns and leaves the room.

"Don't forget to bring sun-friendly clothes. It's summer, not the right time for hoodies."

"Okay," she calls from halfway down the hall. I don't know why I bother. Her and her brother don't leave the house without a sweatshirt of some kind in hand despite the weather.

I turn to the bed and empty out the tote bag I was packing everything into. Most of this stuff we won't need until tomorrow, but I want to get it in the car tonight. If I know my son the way I think I do, he's bound to be running around the house looking for everything and that will make us late.

There are three bottles of sunscreen that I throw into the bag, plus those cooling towels in case any of the boys need it. The only thing I have left to do is pack my clothes for tomorrow, but those will go in a separate bag. I don't want to have to rummage through them to get to what we need at the game.

"Mom!"

What now? This time it's Isaac calling for me. "What do you need?" I finished shoving our items in the tote, and my clothes in my duffel. I throw them over my shoulder and close the door to my room.

"Have you seen my cleats?" I shouldn't have thought anything. I'm pretty sure I brought this on.

"No." I set the bags on the sofa. "Did you check the garage?"

My dad usually makes him leave them out there if they are dusty so he doesn't track the dirt throughout the house.

"That's where I am. They aren't here." This child will be the death of me. Maybe I'm not ready for him to start driving. He'll constantly be asking me to look for his keys.

I glance around the living room to see if I can spy them anywhere. They aren't by the front door where I usually trip over them. I rush to the kitchen, and they aren't by the back door either. We have to leave in ten minutes. I don't have time to go by the store and buy him another pair.

There's only one more place they could be. I hurry back to the living room, and turn on the flashlight on my phone. Getting down on all fours I check under the couch. "Found them."

He runs into the living. "Thanks. I ended up not wearing them to practice last night because I couldn't find them and Coach made me run."

"Maybe put them where they are supposed to go."

"I will." He glances at the clock. "We have to leave or we won't be there early."

"I was waiting on you."

"I have a good feeling about this tournament." He grabs his baseball bag and I get the other bags. "We're bringing home a trophy."

"Dad, you coming?" I call out as we make our way to the garage.

"I'll meet you there. I'm waiting to make sure Abby makes it out okay."

How did he— who am I kidding? He probably knew before I did. At least they know they have people to go to regardless of which parent, or grandparent, it is.

* * *

We did not in fact win any games last night. I'm not sure what happened, but the boys didn't play the way they usually do. There were missed catches, balls they had no business swinging at, and miscommunication all over the field. It's like they forgot how to play baseball.

Keith is on his way to the game with Abby in tow. From the texts she sent me last night, it looks like there's going to be a lot of hurt feelings on the team this year. The coach is shuffling them all around and they won't be playing with their friends. I'll have to ask her for more information when they get to the game.

"Is Grandpa on his way?" Isaac asks from the front seat as we pull into the sports complex.

"Yeah. He should be right behind us. I think he was stopping to get breakfast for us and sports drinks for y'all."

"Good. He'll be here during warmups."

"Why does that matter?" I glance at him from the corner of my eye. I have to keep my eyes on the road at all times because kids dart out from between cars without looking both ways. It's one of my pet peeves.

"Because he didn't make it until the beginning of the first inning last night, and I know that's why we didn't do as well."

"What is he? A team mascot?" Good grief, if he finds this out, his ego will never stop.

"More like a good luck charm." He fiddles with the door handle as I put the car in park.

"Way to make your mom feel special." I laugh so he knows I'm joking. Baseball has never been my thing, but I've learned it over the years since he started playing.

"You are special." He grins at me and opens the door. "You bring all the good snacks." He rushes out of the car with his bag in hand and runs toward the field.

There are worse things, I guess. I could be one of the parents who doesn't show up to anything. There are extenuating circumstances for everything, I know that, but I always want to be in the stands when the kids look up. Despite what other people think, they always do.

I grab the bag with the snacks and the other bag with the sunscreen and carry one on each shoulder to the stands. The one perk of having a kid that likes to be the first one to warm ups is I always get a good spot on the bleachers. Which also means I don't have to lug around chairs everywhere we play.

I place the bags far enough on the bench I'm on to save a seat for Abby, Keith, and Dad. Some of the parents grumble when they see the bags, but I don't care. We all sit together.

Dad is the first one to show up with a bag in each hand. One with food and the other drinks for the bows. "Take this," he hands me a bag. "I'll take this other one to the coach."

I rummage through the bag, pulling out the breakfast tacos I like and leave the rest for the other three to fight over. Opening up the potato and egg taco and adding salsa. It's the best way to eat them.

"I see you've already gotten what you want." Keith's voice scares me and I barely catch my taco before it falls to the ground.

"You should learn to make a sound when you approach," I glare at him as I take a bite. "And yes, I did. If y'all wanted dibs, you should have gotten here earlier."

"We weren't even that far behind, Mom." Abby shakes her head and grabs a couple of tacos. "We were trying to find a close parking spot when we saw Grandpa get out of his car."

"Walk faster," I mumble around a mouthful of food.

Keith's only response is to shake his head. He watches our daughter put her earbuds in and get lost in her phone before turning to me. "So how are things with the new boyfriend?"

"I don't know." I shrug my shoulders and take another bit to give myself time. "We've talked a little bit, but mostly about work."

"I'm sorry."

"No, you're not."

"Let's just say I had higher hopes from him." He pulls out a taco and takes the salsa from me. "You two looked really happy when we saw you. Even if you had a deer in headlights expression from seeing us."

"Not my finest moment."

"It happens," he shrugs and adds the salsa to this taco. "Maybe y'all can work things out. I know the kids didn't fully know at the time, but he seemed to get along with them. Isaac kept telling me about Eric's little brother and how they have similar sports schedules."

Wow. That's something I didn't know. Eric told me he talked about his brother, but not much else. Figuring things out is something I hope we can do. Despite what anyone might think, he fits into our odd family unit.

Dad hurries over to the bleachers and takes a seat next to me, forcing the others to scoot over. "The game is about to start."

"You know they've decided you're their good luck charm, right?"

"Why wouldn't they? I'm amazing." And there goes his ego.

We stop all talk of boyfriends, and good luck charms. Abby takes her earbuds out of her ears, and our focus is on Isaac. He still has a good feeling about the tournament today and I hope like hell it's right.

* * *

We won, and I slide off the bench, gathering our trash to throw away. "It's time to be the snack mom. The team is huddled in between two fields celebrating their victory while the coach tries to calm them down. It's one game and they still have more to play today.

I'm passing out snacks when I catch sight of someone I didn't expect to see for a few more hours. What in the world is Eric doing here? How did he know where we were playing? I didn't give that information when I asked for last night off work.

I hand the bag of snacks to another mom. "Can you finish passing these out?"

"Sure thing." She gladly takes over. Little does she know; those boys are feral when it comes to the snacks.

My feet carry me toward Eric at a pace I didn't realize I had. He has two bouquets of flowers in one hand. His other hand holds something else, but I can't tell what it is. "What are you doing here?"

He looks down at the ground for a few moments, working out what he's going to say. If I didn't know him so well, I would have thought he was ignoring me.

"I, um, came to apologize for being a jerk the other day." He shifts one bouquet to his other hand, and holds the bigger one out to me. "Forgive me?"

"You thought coming to my son's game and doing this in a public space was the right way to go about this?" I hope like hell nobody is paying attention to us. I don't want to be a part of any sort of gossip.

"I was actually going to do it when you came in to work tonight. But he," he nods toward Keith, "paid me a visit. I've been trying to work out how to do this all week. Isaac has some pretty mad skills with a bat by the way."

"How long have you been here?"

"Keith also called the bar last night to let me know what time they were playing this morning. I got here just as it was starting." He's still holding the flowers out to me, and I grab them. "I had to wait for Caroline to get to the flower shop so I could get these, otherwise I would have been here earlier."

"Don't you have to work today?" I don't know why I'm asking him five hundred questions. He's here...and trying to apologize. With the help of my ex-husband, but at least I know they can get along when it matters.

"Lisa's got it. I don't have to be in until you get there. Manager perk." He grins and I remember why I fell for him in the first place despite trying to fight my attraction.

"How do I know you won't walk away next time we have a difficult conversation?" I refuse to hold things back because they are hard. It's why Keith and I didn't work in the end. Too many pent-up emotions. We're better off as friends, but that's beside the point.

"Short answer...you don't. But I'll do my best to hear you out. I got caught up in my feelings. When you didn't tell your kids when you said you would, I assumed that meant the end for us. That I wasn't as important to you as you are to me."

A part of me figured that's what was happening. "You realize this could have been avoided if you would have talked to me, instead of the radio silence other than work related things."

"The phone works both ways." Damn it. He's right. "Please forgive me?"

"Fine," I roll my eyes. "But no more of the sneaky crap behind my back with my ex-husband. It's weird."

"I have to tell you. I'm kind of scared of him."

"You shouldn't be." I shoot a glare over at the person in question and he grins wide. These two are insufferable. "He just wants what is best for all of us. Isaac and Abby are his kids too."

"I know. Which is why I have a lot of respect for him."

Both kids realize he's here at the same time and they rush toward us. "Hey, I didn't know you'd be here today. Is your brother with you?" Of course, Isaac would be worried about that.

"Not today. He had basketball practice this morning." He glances around to make sure we don't have an audience. "But there is something I want to talk to y'all about. I heard your mom told you we're dating." Both kids nod. "What I failed to do is ask if it's okay. I know y'all are older, but you need to know I'm in love with your mom and I don't plan on going anywhere. I'd love to get to know both of you better."

"Gross." Isaac groans. "We did not need to know that."

Maybe he didn't, but I can see the small smile on Abby's face. She needed to know that he was serious about me and them. I'm still reeling over his confession. He told my children he loves me.

"I'm sorry, I'll try to keep the PDA to a minimum. But I do want to get to know y'all better." He hands the flowers to Abby and she gives him a quick hug before stepping back. "So, I got the four of us tickets to a baseball game in a few weeks. And we have tickets to a volleyball game in Dallas."

"Really?" Both kids say in unison.

"Absolutely."

"Thank you." Abby gives him another hug before returning to her dad to tell him all about it. Isaac gives him a nod and runs back to his teammates.

"So, you love me?" I move beside him and lean my head on his shoulder.

"I think that goes without saying."

"Good to know." Turning until I'm in front of him, I wrap my arms around his neck. "Because despite my best efforts, I'm pretty sure I love you, too."

He doesn't hesitate. He pulls me closer to him and his lips crash into mine. This right here feels perfect. Like we were always meant to be.

"Hey," Isaac calls out, and we pull apart. "You said no PDA."

"Sorry," Eric yells back. To me, he whispers, "we'll continue that when we're alone."

"I'll tell my dad he has kid duty tonight and not to expect me until late."

"Good idea." His hand slides down to mine and I lead him back toward the bleachers. There will be obstacles in the future, but I have no doubt we'll overcome them.

epilogue

IT'S BEEN a shaky couple of months. Not because the kids aren't happy to have me around. But because school has started up again and the stay-at-home moms are at the bar again. Not drinking, but getting some time out of the house with their friends. I don't' think they realize it's a lot cheaper if they just go to each other's houses, but that's not my business. Luckily, I don't have to deal with it again until tomorrow.

Today is going to be a fantastic day, though. The state fair is open and all of us are going. Not just me, Joan, and the kids. Keith and her dad will be going along with my mom and brother. It's a family affair and the first time all of us will be in the same space at the same time.

Joan and the kids are staying at my house tonight since they don't have school tomorrow, and Joan doesn't have to work. I've already told Angie I won't be at the staff meeting in the morning, and she didn't give me hell for it. I guess they are as invested in this working as I am.

The kids are in my spare room, arguing about who knows what. Sometimes I think they like to annoy each other to see who gives in first. Joan is in the kitchen, packing a bag.

"What are you doing? We aren't moving to the fair." I lift up a bottle of sunscreen.

"Just taking some essentials. It's hot outside and the sun can be a beating."

"This is your baseball game kit, isn't it?"

"Yep. And have you seen me sunburnt from it?"

"Well, there was—" She cuts my words off with a kiss.

"I was frazzled that day. It's not my fault." She throws everything into a small backpack, and moves it to her shoulders. "Are y'all ready?"

They run out of the room in response, pushing each other out of the way. I lean down to Joan's ear, "Will they fight like this the whole time?"

"You have a little brother, what do you think?" Damn, it's going to be a long day. It'll be worth it, though. "In the car guys."

They pile in the backseat of my car, and I open the car door for Joan. Once she's inside, I close the door and round the car to get behind the wheel. "Any chance you want to practice driving?" My eyes meet Isaac's in the review.

"Please for the love of all things Holy, do not let him drive," Abby argues. "I want to make it to the fair alive."

"Can I?" Isaac's eyes widen. "I've been practicing with Dad."

"Not a chance," Joan answers from the passenger seat. "The traffic will be too bad around the fair." She watches Isaac's shoulders sag. "It's not that I don't trust you. I don't trust the millions of other drivers on the road."

Nice try. He knows as well as I do that it's crap. "If we get back early enough, I'll take you driving around town."

Joan glares at me, but at least she isn't the one who has

to be in the car with him. He actually seems like he wants to learn now. I'm happy to step in and take that burden off her shoulders.

"Really?" Isaacs leans forward waiting for my answer.

"Absolutely." I click my seatbelt in place and everyone else does the same. "We can grab dinner after we drop off the ladies."

"Bet." He leans back and with a grin on his face. I'm not sure if this is the smart move or not, but I'm willing to take that chance. Maybe he won't be as nervous with someone who isn't a parent.

I put the car in reverse, and Joan places her hand over mine to get my attention. She should know she doesn't have to do that. I'm always aware of her. Have been since the first time I saw her. "Thank you," she mouths.

Backing out of the driveway, she keeps a steady grip on my hand. Once I'm out, I put the car in drive and turn my hand until it's clasping hers. Most people aren't looking for the white picket fence at my age, but I'm happy I'm no longer searching for it. I went from someone who doesn't take anything seriously to having a family. I wouldn't want it any other way.

Want to see what Patrick is going through? Grab Hurricanes & Halloween in the Once Upon a Halloween Night Anthology! And keep reading for a sneak peak!

***

Today is the last day I can respond. Yes or no...

There aren't any other surfaces for me to clean. The

freezer is stocked and there isn't really a reason for me to be here. It's only an excuse so I don't have to answer my friends back home. They haven't stopped texting, and calling, since the invites were sent out.

"Why are you staring at your phone like it's a bomb about to blow up in your face?" Eric asks from the kitchen door.

I didn't even hear it open. Or, he's just that sneaky. He really needs a bell around his neck so we know when he's coming.

"I have to RSVP for my high school reunion." It's the one thing that's been plaguing my mind for months. I haven't been home in years, and the only thing keeping me away is my own fear. Fear of seeing her again. It's my own fault, but that's beside the point.

"That doesn't seem like a difficult decision." He is right behind me now. "You either want to, or you don't."

"Why are you even here?" He never comes back here unless he wants me to make him something to go, or watch me over my shoulder.

It's only now that I've noticed the bar is quiet. "We're done with the cleanup, and ready to lock everything down. I didn't see you leave, and assumed you were still in here."

"Sorry, I'm ready to go." I glance toward the freezer I was looking in a few moments ago. "Just making sure I have everything I need for the next couple of days."

"Is this reunion the reason you've been staying late? And helping clean up?"

Always trying to get to the bottom of things, this one. There's no use avoiding the question, he'll keep pestering. "Yeah."

"If it's causing you this much stress, I say don't go. But you could always flip a coin and leave it to fate." He turns toward the door and walks out. Guess I'm locking up tonight. He does have a point though.

Digging around in my pocket, I listen for everyone to leave. The bar is quiet and I take a deep breath. At least nobody will be around to see me do this. Finally, a coin slips through the keys in my pocket, and I pull it out. This small piece of silver will decide if I go to the reunion, or not. Placing it on my thumb, I flick it into the air.

acknowledgments

It goes without saying that writing a book takes a village. I wouldn't have finished this book without my support system.

Steph, thanks for always being my cheerleader when I need to get the words in. One day we'll get to hang out in person instead of online.

Wee One...you kept me on track. The periodic bugging me to make sure I'm writing is exactly the push I needed when I'd rather binge watch my shows.

Hubs & Boy Child, thank you for not talking to me when y'all knew I was writing. That's seriously the best gift ever. And Baby E, you are the cutest distraction when I need a break. Being your gamaw is the biggest honor.

To my Patron, Cindy. Your unwavering support means more than you could ever know.

Readers, bloggers, and anyone else who picks up my books. Thank you! You have no idea how much you reading my words means to me. I couldn't do this without your support. Your excitement keeps me going.

also by katrina marie

Out of the Ashes

Cocktails & Crushes

Brews & Bartenders

Mai Tais & Mistletoe

Martinis & Musicians

Gin & Good Guys

Hurricanes & Halloween

(Once Upon a Halloween Night Anthology)

The Taking Chances Series

Welcome to Your Life

Cruel and Beautiful World

Ways to Go

Remember That Night

My Only Wish is You

From This Moment

Shoot Down the Stars

Love Will Save Your Soul

Take a Chance

Gone in Love Series

Gone Country

Gone Steady

Gone Again

Cocky Hero Club

Big Baller

Silverwood Bulldog Series

Baseball & Broadway

about the author

Katrina Marie lives in the Dallas area with her husband, two children, grand baby, and fur baby. She is a lover of all things geeky and nerdy. When she's not writing you can find her at her daughter's sporting events, playing with the grand, or curled up reading a book.

You can find Katrina Marie online in the following places:

Sign up for my newsletter: https://www.subscribepage.com/KatrinaMarieNewsletter

Website: katrinamarieauthor.com

facebook.com/katrinamarieauthor

twitter.com/katmarieauthor

instagram.com/katrinamarieauthor

bookbub.com/profile/katrina-marie

pinterest.com/katrinamarieauthor

tiktok.com/@katrinamarieauthor

patreon.com/katrinamarie